RIDE OR DIE CHICK 2

Wanda

by

J.M. BENJAMIN

Cover design by Mike J. Rush
Cover Photograph(s): J'Adore Magazine
Interior Design by Nancey Flowers
Edited by Chandra Sparks Taylor–www.chandrasparkstaylor.com

First Flowers in Bloom trade paperback printing 2009

For more information, or to contact the author, send correspondence to:

Flowers in Bloom Publishing, Inc.
2152 Ralph Avenue - #421
Brooklyn, New York 11234
www.flowersinbloompublishing.com

Library of Congress Cataloging-in-Publication Data
Benjamin, J.M.
        Down in the Dirty/ J.M. Benjamin - 1st ed.

ISBN-10: 0979861411

ISBN-13: 978-0979861413

10 9 8 7 6 5 4 3 2
First Paperback Edition

Printed in Canada

ACKNOWLEDGMENTS

Eternal thanks to The Most High for allowing me the strength to keep moving forward and never looking backward. Without Your guidance I would be lost.

Thanks to my family and few friends who have been and continue to be a major asset and supporter in all that I do. I wish you all nothing but the best.

Thanks to all of my readers, old and new. Without you I would not have a voice in this game.

Much love to the many incarcerated men and women around the world who may or may not have read a J.M. Benjamin book. My story behind the stories I write is your story. Continue to believe there are better days ahead because there really is life after incarceration.

Peace,

—J.M.Benjamin

SMITH

7-6-2010

DEDICATION

This book is dedicated to all the women who stand by the men they love.

—J.M.Benjamin

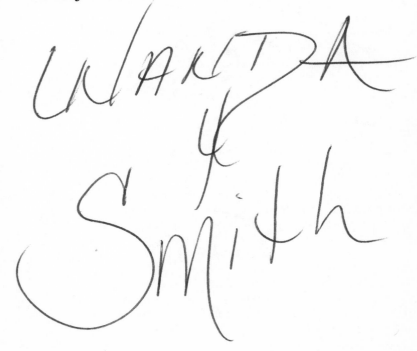

WANDA SMITH

7. 6-2010

RIDE OR DIE CHICK 2

Wanda Smith

a novel
by

J.M. BENJAMIN

SMITH

PROLOGUE

Her vision was blurry as she opened her eyes. She had been under heavy observation for the past four days, expected not to survive. It had been a crucial and life-threatening four days, but being the strong individual she was, she had survived, although she felt a little weak. She had no clue where she was, not even aware that she was unconscious for nearly a week. Upon gaining some of her sight, she began trying to focus on where she actually was. She attempted to wipe her heavy eyelids, feeling the coal on them, which made it difficult to clear her vision, but she came up with a short hand, realizing she had been handcuffed to something.

With her free hand she wiped her eyes, and as her vision became clearer she noticed she was connected to a hospital bed. But that was not all. She had a tube stuck in her chained-up arm, and it ran from a machine, along with another one under her hospital gown. For the life of her she couldn't figure out how she wound up in a hospital cuffed to a bed. Her memory was a blur, and she had no recollection of what had taken place days ago. She began moving only to find out her entire body was sore. But, why? She had no clue.

She continued looking around, searching for clues that would give her some indication how she got into this predicament. As she looked to her left, she spotted a newspaper on the hospital night stand next to the bed. She painfully reached over and grabbed the paper. The date read October 28, 2007, and she couldn't determine whether the newspaper was actually today's date or yesterday. The front page had a heading that stuck out to her, but she didn't know why. It read in big bold letters, The Bonnie and Clyde of the New Millennium. Under the heading was a picture of a black Mercedes CLS. Even before she began reading the article the car triggered something inside her. Within the first four lines tears began to roll down her face. Reading her soul mate's name caused Teflon to regain all of her senses and have her thoughts restored. Everything now all made sense. October 28 was the day they decided to rob the bank, the heading Bonnie and Clyde of the new millennium referred to her and Treacherous; the Mercedes was the car she and Treacherous had jacked and murdered the two young dealers for to use on the bank job. She had taken a shot to the side as they were coming out of the bank, and Treacherous had taken the police on a high-speed chase in an attempt to get her to the hospital, which was all she could remember. As she continued to read, the rest was answered for her in black and white. Treacherous had gone all out right there on the Virginia Beach exit while she lay unconscious.

Teflon's tears flowed harder as she envisioned the scene. She knew there was only one thing that no one else could know besides her that would make Treacherous take the route he did. He thought she was dead. How could he have thought she was dead? she wondered. Was her pulse or heartbeat that low that it went undetected? Teflon wanted to know the answers to those questions because they were the answers that caused her to lose her other half, or her better half as Treacherous would say. She smiled at the thought. She remembered when Treacherous had first told her about the bank and how he had said that after that day every dude and chick would be comparing themselves to us. He said they were like Bonnie and Clyde and Romeo and Juliet all wrapped up in one, only harder, and everything he said was coming to pass. Teflon herself had viewed their love for each other as a Romeo and Juliet relationship because they too were young and in love, and just as Romeo took his own life assuming Juliet died, Treacherous had basically done the same, and just as Juliet woke only to find out that Romeo was dead, so did Teflon. She began beating herself up knowing had she not been unconscious, she and Treacherous would have gone out together in a blaze of glory. She began ripping the tubes from herself in an attempt to find a way to take her own life, just as Juliet did, so she could meet up with her soul mate again.

While in the process of doing all of this, the doctor walked, catching Teflon in the act and rushed over to her.

"Ms. Jackson!" the doctor yelled, grabbing her free hand. "Calm down. You're alright. You and the baby are going to be fine. Just take it easy."

Up until his last statement Teflon continued to resist the doctor's attempts to restrain her, but hearing what he just said registered enough to get her to instantly stop what she was trying to do.

"What did you just say?" she asked, making sure she had heard him correctly as she cleared her throat.

"I said to take it easy, you and the baby are going to be fine," he repeated. Suddenly Teflon noticed the officer guarding her room stick his head inside the door.

"Is everything alright, doc?" the white young-looking officer asked, hearing all the commotion.

"Yes, everything is fine," the doctor replied not wanting to cause a scene.

By now, Teflon had calmed down completely after getting the doctor's confirmation on his last statement.

"That's better," expressed the doctor as he started reattaching the tubes that Teflon had ripped out.

He assumed she had awakened and wigged out at the sight of everything, which he thought was normal in her case since experiencing such a traumatic event days ago. He couldn't believe how such a beautiful-looking woman could be mixed up in such an ugly ordeal and have dealings with a man of the young man's caliber that he had read about in the newspaper and had seen plastered all over the news. If he had he known the extent of their bond and relationship he would not have been so quick to doubt Teflon's ruthlessness. He had left the newspaper on the nightstand next to her bed so she could see it when she awoke. He figured she would want to know the outcome of the serious situation she had just survived, that he felt she was probably forced into. How could she have gone along with such a plan on her own free will as innocent as she appeared to look? Since he grew up with practically a silver spoon in his mouth and was naïve as green as artificial grass when it came to the streets.

"It's good to see you awake," he said. "We thought we were going to lose you, but you've proved you're a strong young woman."

Teflon watched him as his hand slid under the hospital blanket with the intent of reconnecting the tube that was once stuck in her side. She felt his hand brush up against her bare hip and flinched. No man besides Treacherous had touched her body in over twelve years, and the thought of the doctor's foreign hand on her sent chills through her body.

"I got it," she said, moving the doctor's hand away.

"Oh, I'm sorry," said the doctor, thinking he had hurt her. "Are you sore?"

"Yeah, a little."

"Alright. I'll see to it that you get something to help with the pain and for infections as well. You took a nasty hit. It was touch and go in the operating room."

"How long was I unconscious?" Teflon asked.

"Four days."

"Damn. What about the baby? How long have I been pregnant?" she asked.

"You mean you didn't know?" the doctor asked, surprised.

"If I did, I wouldn't have asked," Teflon replied and was becoming agitated.

The doctor caught the hostility mixed with sarcasm and blamed it on Teflon's condition.

"You're five weeks pregnant."

Teflon thought back to the last time she and Treacherous had made love and began to smile at the memory, while tears streamed down her face once again. Their last encounter was the time she had awakened, only to find Treacherous masturbating with one hand while he had his other one between her thighs. She remembered all too well and realized that had she not replaced his hand with her love box that day, she would not have a part of him growing inside of her. Adding this new piece to the equation caused

Teflon to rethink her plans. There was nothing else she wanted more in life than to join Treacherous wherever he was, whether it be heaven or hell, but now because of the five-week-old life that dwelled inside of her, her plans to meet up with her better half would have to be delayed and their reunion would have to be put on hold, at least for another seven months.

CHAPTER ONE

"All rise for the Honorable Judge William H. Braswell of the District of Virginia."

Teflon sighed in frustration as she struggled to lift herself up out of the wooden courtroom chair. She was sick and tired of being lugged back and forth to court month after month for something she already knew what the final outcome would be. She felt it had been a long, drawn-out case. When she first laid eyes on the jurors who would determine her fate, there was no doubt in her mind what type of verdict would be handed down. Seeing them over to her far right now, and the way they stared and murmured among themselves only confirmed Teflon's thoughts. The only reason she had actually taken her case to trial was because she knew it was what Treacherous would have wanted her to do.

"We fighters, babe. We go hard or go home," he would always say to her, Teflon recalled. She fought to suppress her emotions at the thought of her other half as a sharp pain jolted through the small of her back. Between the spasms she had been having since the gunshot wound from which she was recovering and the nine-month-old life growing inside of her, her movement was turtle like and painful. As tough as she was, she was no match for the battle she was going through with the life inside of her. Her attorney made an attempt to aid her. It was apparent that she was in pain, but he was stopped in his tracks by Teflon's sudden expression, which spoke volumes, making it perfectly clear that his services were not welcomed or needed. After representing her for the last eight months, Teflon maintained her nonchalant and cold demeanor, so he shouldn't have been surprised by her refusal for help.

Teflon stood in front of the table with her hair pulled back in a ponytail sporting her gray county sweat suit and county-issued tennis shoes. She used the table to brace herself as the judge entered the courtroom. The additional twenty-one pounds she'd put on between the baby and being in jail made it that much more difficult for her to stand. The weight was uncomfortable for her, and she couldn't wait to shed both the extra pounds and the baby and get back to her normal size eight.

"Please be seated," the judge instructed

Teflon grunted as another spasm shot through her lower back.

"This is the trial of the United States of America versus Teflon Jackson. Counsels, state your names for the record."

"Your honor, Mark Stanford of the public defender's office of Norfolk for the defense," announced Teflon's attorney.

"Christopher Malloy, District Attorney of Norfolk for the prosecution, your honor."

"If I'm correct, today is the final day of this trial," the judge stated, skimming through the paperwork before him. "Counsels will deliver their closing arguments and remarks, and the jury will render a verdict based on the information and evidence that has been presented to them throughout this trial. Counsel, are you ready to proceed?"

"Yes, your honor," they both replied.

"Mr. Stanford."

This was the moment of the truth, Mark Stanford thought. He took one look back at Teflon and slightly shook his head in disbelief as he sighed to himself. In exchange, Teflon stared him straight in the eyes, unfazed by his sympathetic look back. He couldn't believe how hard core Teflon was and had been throughout his entire representation. In his thirteen years of practice as a public defender, he had never encountered a client more difficult and rebellious than Teflon Jackson. In the eight months he had been her lawyer she was uncooperative. It was like pulling teeth trying to get her to open up and assist him. According to what he had read and discovered about the case, he knew her fate was inevitable. She would receive a lengthy prison sentence. There were a few angles and approaches he would have liked to have taken for her defense, but Teflon refused to talk with him after stating she wanted to go to trial. She wouldn't budge, even when he tried to appeal to her maternal side she rejected the notion of helping him help her. Now his only defense was based on the lack of evidence they actually had against her. Mark sympathized with the pregnant young woman, but due to his heavy workload and promising cases of clients who were willing to help themselves as well as the government in exchange for leniency, he was all too happy to bring this particular case to a close. Mark took a sip of the ice water that sat before him and cleared his throat.

"Members of the jury," he stated as he walked from behind the court table and adjusted his tricolor neck tie. "In the past few months you have heard allegations from the prosecution against my client that literally makes her out to look like not only this modern-day Bonnie from the historical Bonnie and Clyde, but also this stone-cold killer. As you know, Ms. Jackson is being charged with multiple counts of conspiracy to commit armed robbery in the first degree and conspiracy to commit murder in the first."

He let the accusations of the charges linger before he continued. "But what she is being accused of and charged with is not the case here today. No." He paused.

"The case here is what evidence has been presented to substantiate these allegations against my client." He paused again then pivoted.

"The prosecution would like you to be convinced that my client, Ms. Teflon Jackson, conspired to commit armed robbery, yet he failed to produce any surveillance video clearly showing my client's direct involvement in the allegation, nor was he able to produce a witness from inside the bank who could testify whether my client was held against her own free will by the diseased Mr. Treacherous Freeman."

The attorney's opening statement and the mere mention of Treacherous' name instantly caught her attention but rubbed Teflon the wrong way. She really didn't care about his closing argument since he portrayed her as the victim and her other half as the villain. She was tempted to jump up and set the record straight, but Treacherous' words danced in her head as if he were right beside her in her ear. "Using emotions over intellect is never justifiable," she heard him repeating.

"Why the fuck you leave me like this?" Teflon silently questioned, staring up to the ceiling as if Treacherous were up there looking down at her. She grabbed a napkin off the table to wipe her left nostril that began to run. She sat up and then became attentive as her lawyer continued. "The prosecution states that my client is guilty of conspiracy to commit *murder,*" her attorney said emphatically, turning to face Teflon, pointing in her direction. He could tell she was not too pleased by the comment he had made about her deceased boyfriend. He knew he was treading on thin ice with her by painting the picture he did, but it was the only way he felt he could help spare her life. He was fully aware of the bond the couple shared. He had found out first hand a few months back, when he had made the fatal mistake of merely referring to Treacherous as *this guy* and mentioned that he is deceased. At forty-three years old, standing at five feet ten inches and tipping the scales at two hundred-fifteen pounds, he had never been so afraid of someone he outweighed and outmatched in his life as he did that day. To top it off, it was a woman who instilled this fear within him. It wasn't anything she had done - but what she had said, and how she said it, that sent chills throughout Mark Stanford's entire body. He couldn't help

but replay the words in his head that invaded his sleep many nights." If you ever speak of my deceased loved one in vein in my presence ever again, you're gonna meet him."

The calm manner in which she spoke convinced him she meant every word of it. His first instinct was to report the incident and abandon the case, but his curiousness overpowered his decision. He wanted to see how this particular case unfolded and wanted to be the one who played a part in how it happened.

"The murder weapons retrieved from the crime scene did not possess my client's fingerprints."

His words caused Teflon to peer over toward the jurors to see their reaction. She noticed a few puzzled and quizzical expressions on a few of their faces. She knew that this key element of her case would stir up some if not a great deal of confusion among them. She was confused about this initially, knowing her involvement like she knew the back of her own hand. As she played the tapes back to the event, there was no doubt in her mind that she had hit at least one of the officers when they came out of Bank of America before she took one in the side. The only possible explanation was that Treacherous had wiped her prints off the gun she used in order to protect her.

Teflon listened as her attorney continued. "Yes, my client is with child and is guilty, but not of the charges she is being accused of." Attorney Stanford paused for a second time to let the statement about Teflon being pregnant marinate. "The only thing my client is guilty of today is loving a man too much and too hard," he said. "And that, ladies and gentlemen, is not why my client is on trial here today. I hope you take all that I've said into account when making your ruling." Attorney Stanford ended with a bow and walked back around the table where Teflon sat. The two exchanged quick glances. Teflon gave her attorney no indication that she approved of his argument and he wasn't looking for one. After all, he was just doing his job. District Attorney Christopher Malloy skimmed through his notes one last time before he stood. He then looked over at Teflon who felt his eyes on her.

"What the fuck you lookin' at?" she mumbled under her breath just enough for him to   hear and read her lips. The DA smiled and pushed his glasses up on his face. He had no sympathy whatsoever for the female criminal who sat across from him. According to the evidence there was no doubt in his mind or heart that Teflon Jackson deserved all that she would receive and then some after a verdict was handed down. Despite what he was able to produce to build a strong case against her, he was confident the jury would render the right decision and continue to keep the female menace to society off the streets. It was DA Malloy's intent to push for the maximum penalties once she was proclaimed guilty. ''

"Ladies and gentlemen of the jury, despite what counsel says, the prosecution failed to produce. Evidence has been presented to you that clearly shows the accused is in fact guilty of the charges for which she stands trial. Evidence showed that Ms. Teflon Jackson and Mr. Treacherous Freeman exited the Norfolk Virginia branch of Bank of America with weapons and were involved in a gun battle with police. Evidence clearly showed that there was a high-speed pursuit for Ms. Jackson and the deceased, endangering the welfare of other pedestrians and law enforcement. Evidence showed that the vehicle used as the get-away car was in fact the same car that was carjacked from a local McDonald's where two murders were committed. Evidence also shows that during this crime spree six state police officers and four federal agents were killed in the line of duty, and five others were wounded. I'm not standing before you trying to convince you to speculate or even try to figure out what I didn't or why I didn't present the evidence counsel said I failed to produce. All I ask is that you review the facts and evidence presented to you and render the decision you feel fits the crime. Thank you."

District Attorney Malloy clasped his hands together and ended with a slight bow to the jury. He then returned to the table opposite Teflon and her attorney. She rolled her eyes at the district attorney as he zipped past her. When he sat down, he looked over at Teflon again. She was busy visualizing and imagining Treacherous pistol whipping him with the butt of his gun while she stood there and watched.

"Members of the jury, you have heard both arguments in the case of The United States of America versus Teflon Jackson. It is your duty after hearing both parties and based on the evidence presented before you that beyond a reasonable doubt, a decision is made. It's now 10:45 A.M. The court will recess for an hour while the jury returns to chambers. Bailiff, please escort the jury back to chambers," the judge ordered, banging the gavel. Hearing that, the two front marshals sitting two rows behind Teflon and her attorney stood and approached the front of the courtroom.

"Ms. Jackson, please stand and turn around," the female marshal requested with handcuffs in hand.

Teflon exhaled and complied. The cuffs were then placed around her wrists.

"Too tight?" the marshal asked.

Teflon answered with a nod.

"I'll be back there to see you shortly," her attorney announced as Teflon was escorted through the court and off to the federal holding cell. She didn't even bother to acknowledge that she had heard his words. Attorney Stanford and the male federal marshal exchanged a mutual glance. In their line of work they were used to detainees acting the way Teflon did.

Teflon was led to the space that became all too familiar over the past few months. The ten by ten holding cell was as dismal as Teflon's mood. Still she knew this cell would probably be a better place than where she'd eventually end up. At least here she was had some privacy.

"Okay, let me get these cuffs off you," the federal marshal said. "I'll be back to check on you periodically, and I'll see if I can get you a pillow or blanket."

Teflon holed on the bullpen's bench slowly made her way to the floor.

The bench was too small and uncomfortable for her so she chose the floor instead, using the edge of the bench for support. Soon, she would receive closure on this chapter of her life. Despite her attorney's best attempt to defend her, Teflon knew she would not be walking up out of her situation scot free—not now, not later. She had come to terms with that. When she felt she could no longer take it, she'd meet up with Treacherous again. She lifted up her sweatshirt and white tee and began rubbing her stomach as images of her last moments with Treacherous flashed through her mind.

"Treach," Teflon had yelled as she pointed her 380 and nine-millimeter butler in the direction of the police and began squeezing the triggers.

"Babe, get in!" Treacherous yelled over to Teflon, attempting to cover her as police returned fire.

"Treach, I'm losing a lot of blood," Teflon cried as she applied pressure to the right side of her hip in attempt to minimize the bleeding.

"Just hold on, boo. I got you. You gonna be a'ight. We gonna make it up outta this shit, and I'ma get you to a hospital. Tef? Tef?"

"Huh?"

"Wake up, baby. Don't fall asleep. Stay awake, you hear me?"

Teflon could feel him rubbing her hair. "Daddy, I'm weak, and it's cold."

"Tef! Man the fuck up. You a'ight? Shake that shit off. Stop all that mu'fuckin whinin' and shit, and man the fuck up."

"Who the fuck you yellin' at, boy?"

"Boo, my bad. Don't talk. Save your strength," Treacherous said, moving Teflon's hair from out of her face. "Don't start bitchin' up now, mufucka." Despite her condition, she managed to smile.

"Fuck you." Treacherous smiled back.

"Boo, hold on. We're almost there." Teflon heard Treacherous' words but could not respond. She was slipping in and out of consciousness.

"Tef," she heard her lover call out again but still she was unable to respond. Treacherous' voice was muffled, and his words became inaudible.

"Teflon!" was the last word she heard before she lost full consciousness.

"Ms. Jackson." Hearing her name snapped Teflon out of her daze. When she looked up her lawyer was standing outside the holding cell. She raised her sweatshirt and wiped her entire face. Her trip down memory lane made her emotional. She was mad at herself for allowing her attorney to witness her in that state. Out of respect, Mark Stanford pretended not to notice by going through his cellular phone for no particular reason. Teflon made an effort to stand up.

"No please, don't get up," he said. "I was just coming to let you know that the jury should be returning in about twenty minutes. The marshal will be here to get you in about ten. Honestly, I have to say, Ms. Jackson, I have a good feeling about this case. I think the jury may possibly rule in your favor."

Teflon looked at her attorney and cut her eyes and turned her head in the opposite direction. Who the fuck was he really trying to convince? With the exception of the Hispanic man and the black woman, the rest of the jurors were lily white. She knew her fate even before it was handed down to her. She was disgusted at him for lying in her face. He didn't even look like he believed the words coming out of his mouth.

"I'll see you back in the courtroom," he remarked dryly, shaking his head in disbelief about how nonchalant she was at a time like this.

***

"Has the jury reached a verdict?"

"Yes we have, your honor," a middle-age white female juror replied.

"Ms. Jackson, please face the jury." Teflon slightly turned her head toward the jury. The judge shot her a look of disgust.

"Ms. Jackson, please turn and face the jury," he said.

Teflon sucked her teeth and shifted toward the jury.

"Juror number one, please stand and read your verdict." The juror stood and unfolded a white piece of paper, faced the judge, then began to read.

"We the jurors, in the case of the United States of America versus Teflon Jackson, find that on the charges of conspiracy to commit armed robbery in the first degree on counts one three sixteen, we find the defendant," she paused, turning her attention to Teflon, "guilty on all counts."

Teflon's lawyer dropped his head and placed it in the palm of his hand. Teflon only smirked. She was not at all surprised at the verdict. As far as she was concerned the juror did not have to finish.

"On the charges of conspiracy to commit murder in the first degree, on counts one three thirteen, we find the defendant guilty as charged." Just as with the first, the second conviction did not faze Teflon. She had already mentally prepared for the verdicts. After all, she was guilty of the charges for which she stood trial. Life as she knew it was literally over for her the day Treacherous had been taken from her. Besides the life she carried inside her, she had no other reason to live for. Mentally and emotionally she was already dead. No, there was nothing more they could do to her she felt. The DA had a look of victory plastered across his face as he stood.

"Bitch-ass nigga," Teflon murmured just loud enough for the DA to hear as the two made eye contact.

"Your honor, the prosecution is moving to impose the maximum penalties under the federal guidelines against Ms. Jackson," the DA said, breaking his stare with Teflon.

"I object, your honor," Teflon's attorney hopped up and rebutted. "My client…"

"Your client is an unremorseful menace to society and a threat to our community," the DA quickly snapped back, cutting Teflon's attorney short.

"Fuck you, you gay ass muthafucka," Teflon lashed out, insulted by the DA's statement.

"Order," the judge demanded, repeatedly banging his gavel. The marshals rushed toward the potential altercation, as Teflon attempted to rise out of her chair.

"Ms. Jackson, we will not—"

"I don't give a fuck. I don't give a fuck," Teflon screamed as the marshals reached her, before the judge could complete his sentence.

"Calm down, Ms. Jackson," the female marshal advised as she took hold of Teflon's left arm. The other marshal said nothing, grabbing her by her right one.

"Fuck that. Kill me now." The DA put distance between himself and Teflon, fearful of what could possibly happen next. The jurors were bewildered at Teflon's sudden outburst and some became noticeably afraid of the wild woman. They were immediately escorted out of the courtroom.

"I don't give a fuck. Kill...ugh!" Teflon balled over and grabbed her stomach.

"Ms. Jackson, are you okay?" her attorney asked.

"Call the EMT. I think she's going into labor," the female marshal instructed her partner.

Teflon continued to scream in agony. Her cries shook the courtroom walls.

"Holy cow," Teflon's attorney shouted. Everyone's attention was immediately drawn to her lawyer wanting to know what had stifled him.

"She's bleeding." A burgundy stain spread between her legs.

"Where's the EMT? She's hemorrhaging," the female marshal yelled, seeing her partner re-enter the courtroom.

"On their way. Be here in five," he replied.

"Damnit, this doesn't look good. Tell them to hurry," she retorted.

Teflon muttered something to herself.

The female marshal moved in closer to hear Teflon. "Ms. Jackson, I don't understand you. I need you to speak more clearly."

Teflon's mind was elsewhere. The female marshal continued to try to make out her words but wasn't successful. Just as the EMT burst through the courtroom door, the female marshal looked as if she was finally able to decode Teflon's murmurs. To be sure, she moved in closer until Teflon's lips were nearly touching her earlobe.

"Treacherous, I love you," was what she had heard right before Teflon Jackson passed out.

CHAPTER TWO

Teflon awoke to find her wrist handcuffed to a hospital gurney and tubes running from her body to machines. Her body was sore. The scenery was like déjà vu to as she recalled the last time she landed herself in the hospital. This time though, it was different. Teflon remembered going into labor and losing consciousness inside the courtroom. As she reflected, the thought of her and Treacherous' child came to light in her mind. Where was her baby? she wondered. Then it dawned on her. The last words she had heard before she blacked out were that she was hemorrhaging. Her chest began to tighten and her mouth became dry. There was no doubt in her mind she had lost the one thing that would have kept her and Treacherous connected for life. Teflon could not believe she had miscarried as she felt her stomach with her free hand. Something didn't feel right to her. She slid the hospital sheet to the side and hiked the hospital dress up over her waist. When she looked down, Teflon saw that her stomach possessed staples. The realization she had been cut open instantly enraged her. Not only had she lost her child, but she was left with a scar that would remind her of this for the rest of her life. In the nine months she had the little life growing inside of her, Teflon had grown to love her expected arrival despite knowing she would have to detach herself from these feelings, due to her present circumstances. Now there was no need to. Teflon became emotional, bothered by the thought. There had only been three living creatures in the world she had ever loved; her mother, Treacherous, and their unborn child. None of the three existed any longer. With that in mind, just as the last time she ended up in the hospital, Teflon thought about ending her own life. The only reason she had lasted this long was for the baby's sake, and now there was no real reason for her to live any longer. She searched the room, looking for something within reach to aid her in her departure. For the second time, Teflon began snatching the tubes out of herself with her free hand, only to be interrupted by a loud cry.

"Shhh," the young white nurse gently said to the little infant wrapped up in the powder-blue blanket. She was so engulfed quieting the baby she never noticed that Teflon was awake, let alone pulling her tubes out. Teflon's heart skipped a beat when she saw the nurse holding the screaming baby.

"Ooh." By the time the nurse looked up, Teflon had ceased her behavior. "Didn't know you were awake," she remarked over the baby's cries, while rocking the infant in her arms.

"I've been bringing him in here every day for the past few days to see you."

Him, Teflon heard the young nurse say. Hearing she had conceived a boy made her smile on the inside. She was hoping to have a son to carry on his father's legacy. "Look, mommy's awake," she said to Teflon's son.

"He's very handsome," the nurse added, bringing the baby closer to Teflon. One look at her son, and Teflon's heart melted like fried ice cream. For that brief moment, her black heart was replaced with a pin cushion. Upon seeing her son, her maternal instincts kicked in. She felt like a woman— a mother. "Do you want to hold him?" the nurse asked, handing the infant over to Teflon. She cuddled her son with her free hand and looked at him and could see he was the spitting image of Treacherous.

"Little Treach," she whispered. Just as she was about to lift her son to embrace him and give him a kiss, her room door flew up and two federal agents appeared.

"Ma'am, please take the child from the detained," one of the agents instructed. His words snapped Teflon back to reality.

The nurse took hold of Teflon's son. "Sorry," she whispered with a genuinely sympathetic look right before she hurried out of the room. Teflon knew that would be the last time she would see or hold her son again. On the day she was sentenced to 480 months in a West Virginia federal prison, she also signed her son whom she named Treacherous Antwan Freeman Jr. over to the state of Virginia.

CHAPTER THREE

Four years later....

Teflon had just completed her last set of calisthenics-consisting of twenty sets of ten pull- ups, twenty-five push-ups, and twenty dips. She then made her way over to the royal-blue plastic mat to get in her ten sets of a hundred count crunches before she made her way to the track for her cardiovascular workout, consisting of a two-mile daily ritual that she had been following religiously for the past three and a half years. Since being at West Virginia Federal Institution, Teflon had diligently thrown herself into working out, which resulted in a tight body to die for. Her arms were muscular in a feminine way, and her traps and shoulders were toned. Even through the sports bra and the short tee she wore, you could see the separation and perkiness in her full breasts. Her midsection was flat and cut, and the perspiration that glistened over her entire body enhanced the definition in her stomach and highlighted the tattoo she had done of the mugshot of Treacherous from a newspaper clipping during her trial. She also added the words *The Last American Gangsta* replacing the scars she bore from the C-section and gunshot wound. Her waistline was smaller than she could recall, but her hips and ass had spread like smooth butter on hot toast, compliments of the squats and thrusts she'd incorporated into her workout regime.

Straight women envied from afar while gay women lusted from a close distance. They either wanted to be her, be with her, or be around her, but Teflon didn't allow any of those luxuries. She had made it perfectly clear to those who thought it was a game that she was not to be reckoned with and was not there to make friends. During Teflon's first three weeks on the compound, a six-foot dark-skinned, two-hundred-plus-pound manly looking butch from Philadelphia tried to enter the shower with her. At the time, Teflon was preoccupied with washing her face, so the butch slid in undetected. But the foreign touch around her waist and body pressed up against her own wet flesh from behind was enough to trigger her off instantly. Before the brawly woman realized she had made a fatal mistake, Teflon had already slipped out of her grays and rapidly spun around. In one motion, she head butted the butch. Because of the height difference, Teflon's blow was delivered to the woman's nose. The nose crunched loudly on impact as blood sprayed on the shower walls.

By the time the facility rovers arrived, Teflon was sitting on top of the whale of a woman, strangling the life out of her with her towel. Because of her past history with similar incidents, she was transferred to Danbury Federal Correctional Institution in Connecticut. Teflon served six months in lockup and later was returned to general population. "Big Bertha" as she was known was the most feared and highly respected woman on the compound. Word had gotten out that Teflon had beaten Bertha's ass and had also stood trial for the modern-day Bonnie and Clyde case. Both of these things helped her gain respect and fear from her peers.

Teflon dressed in her khaki prison-issued uniform after she had groomed for the day and made her way toward the dayroom. The guards had just completed count for the facility and like clockwork , Teflon hurried to be the first who made it in and out of the shower before mail call. For the past three-and-a-half year's mail call had actually been the highlight of her day in the woman's prison. The letters she received faithfully over the years kept her sanity intact and gave her a reason to want to continue to live. Teflon entered the dayroom just as the officers began pulling the rubber-band stacks of mail out of the big beige mail bag. Teflon stayed in the background, posted up against the dayroom's wall while the officer sounded off with the mail call.

All the other female inmates became accustomed to Teflon positioning herself in the section by the dayroom door and made it their business not to invade her space or take that position in the room.

"Teflon Jackson," the officer called out.

"Right here," Teflon answered, making her way to the front of the room. The dayroom parted like the Red Sea as she navigated to the officer. No one besides the officer ever touched Teflon's mail, and that's the way she wanted it. Teflon retrieved the letter and made her way to her room. She sat on her bottom bunk, removed the contents from the envelope and began to read.

I greet you with the highest salutations of peace and wish you many blessings upon receiving this missive.

Teflon always smiled at the opening remarks. They had always been the same from day one. No other man had ever made her smile like that other than Treacherous, up until that moment. She continued to read.

So how is my daughter-in-law? I know it's a question I already know the answer to, but it's always a beautiful thing to hear it in your own words. As for this ol' man. I'm as strong as an ox and not just physically, but also smart as a fox, sharper than a nail, with patience like a snail. The Creator continues to bless me to live to see and fight another day, just as He is doing for you. By the time you receive this letter, it will officially be my twenty-second year behind these walls, and still my health and sanity are intact. I'm getting closer and closer to seeing daylight at the end of the tunnel. Five-and-a-half more years to go. That's a small thing to a giant like myself. You know, the only reason I speak about time is not to get you to monitor it, but to motivate you to beat it. Don't let 'em win. If I can do it, so can you. We are cut from the same cloth—same fabric, same texture. Utilize this time wisely. When you walk out that door, no matter when it is, because you will, I'll be standing right there waiting for you with open arms, and you can take that to the bank. Smile.

Teflon couldn't help but chuckle to herself. It never failed. He had always slid a joke or pun in reference to a bank in all his letters.

Speaking about utilizing your time wisely, I just finished reading the last four chapters you sent me of your book. Man, sister you sure can write! I know you got some more for me, so I'm waiting. It's not only enjoyable, it's also powerful and emotional, three things that comprise a good book, and I'm not just saying that because you're the writer and it's about you and my son. I know I've said it before and you tell me to stop saying it, but I appreciate you sharing your past with me through these chapters and for allowing me the opportunity to know things about my son that I never knew and he would never offer to share. The two of you have indeed been through hell and back. You two remind me so much of Teresa and me. I know you were thinking about changing the title of the book, but I think it's appropriate. It doesn't get any better than The Story of Treacherous and Teflon. *It wouldn't make sense to name it anything else. I hope you reconsider and keep that. Still no news about the whereabouts of my grandson? The system is crazy. Don't worry, though. As promised, the first foot I step outside these walls I will be on my J-O-B getting some answers. Like I told you before, I gave you my word that I will find Little Treach if he's anywhere in the State of Virginia. With that being said, until our pens meet paper again, which in our case will be the following day, stay strong, stay focused, and stay blessed.*

Always Yours Truly,
R. Robinson

Teflon finished reading the letter and placed it back in the envelope.

Six days a week for over three years, she had been receiving letters from Treacherous' father. She remembered how skeptical and hesitant she was when another female inmate from Virginia Beach approached her with the letter from Richie Gunz. The first time it was brought to her she refused to accept it. Two days later, she sought out the girl and found that she still possessed it. When she read it, the letter brought tears to her eyes. She was so overwhelmed, it took her a week before she could respond. When she finally did reply, it opened up a line of communication and a bond that Teflon knew would last forever. Sometimes when she read Richie's letters, his words reminded her so much of Treacherous. She could see where Treacherous had gotten his strength and the natural command for respect. She enjoyed hearing from him just as much as she enjoyed writing back. It was he who suggested she write about her relationship with Treacherous and how their bond was formed. It seemed like a crazy idea at first. Then one mysterious night a year ago, she dreamed about her and Treacherous' lives from the day they first met in the Norfolk Detention Center, up until the time of his demise. It was that very same night she woke up and poured her emotions onto paper.

Teflon put the letter in her locker and retrieved her Walkman along with her notepad and pen. She had been thinking all day about penning the new chapter and intended to write this evening. Each chapter written thus far had been emotional for her because it reminded her of the past. She opened up her notepad and began to write.

Chapter Fourteen: For the Love of Riding

Bikes, all shapes and sizes and colors—from Ducattis, Hiabusas, R1's, CBRs, Suzukis to Yamahas flooded the streets for the Richmond Gold Bowl weekend, held at Virginia Union's football stadium. Male and female riders displayed bike trucks and stunts such as indos, burn-outs, 360s pop-up wheelies, standing up and bunny hops with and without backseat passengers. Asses twice the size of mine with mere G-strings and thongs rode on the backs of their boyfriends' and girlfriends' street machines as they raced and performed for onlookers and fellow bikers.

Treacherous and I blended in like chameleons as we rode along side of each other with our customized bikes and matching helmets. Between our outfits and what we invested into our babies, we had an estimated value easily of a hundred grand. Between the chrome pipes, alloy rims, customized seats, and original bodies, our bikes were a sight to see. This was the first time Treacherous and I had bought these particular bikes out for public display. We normally used our R1's or Ducattis when we were putting in work, but due to the distance between Richmond and where we lived in Tide Water, Treacherous wanted the most powerful bikes we possessed to pull off the score.

Our bikes had parts from the Hiabusas, R1's, and Ducattis, we

called them "HARDS." We scanned the area for at least three hours
before we finally zeroed in on some potential prospects, and potential
they had. The people next to us definitely had the hottest bikes out that
night. Not to mention the fact that they had the most jewelry on and
the most females flocking around them. To us, that meant money. The
way these jokers looked there was no doubt they were packing paper,
judging by the gold digging females lingering in the area. They were
posted up on the side of Virginia Union Stadium rotating at least ten
blunts in the cipher of bikers and groupies, while throwing back cans
of Bud Light and white liquor. There were six of them total. Their bikes
had Texas plates. It was plain to see that the largest of the six with the
opened leather biker vest,revealing his Chia Pet chest and one too
many kegs of beer belly was the head man of the crew. Both Treacherous and I gave each other knowing looks. We had come across licks
like this countless times, so how we handled it would be no different.

"Ready, babe?" Treacherous asked, already knowing the answer
to his own question. He knew I hated when he asked me that, and he
did it on purpose to get a spark out of me. As always, I ignored his
question and shot it right back at him.

"You ready?"

He smirked and drew one of his two silencer weapons from behind. I did the same as we rode up on the small bike party.

The first shot Treacherous delivered split the leader's head like a
cornrow part. The second and third ones tore into his midsection in
succession like darts in a bull's eye. The groupie nearest let out a loud
scream only to be silenced by the barrel of my glock 40. Thanks to the
loud music and other partygoers her cries went unnoticed. Before
anyone could make any sudden moves, Treacherous and I had already secured the perimeter. Everyone was oblivious as to what was
taking place over at the blindsided area where the Texas bikers were
posted up.

"If you don't wanna end up like this fat mu'fucka here you better
come up off every mu'fuckin' thing you got from your neck down.
Think it's a game," Treacherous said, growling.

"Shut the fuck up," I told the groupie. "You ain't got shit we want."

Out of fear they silenced themselves. Quickly the other five bikers began unassing themselves of all of their prize possessions and monies, and they started dumping it in the knap sack Treacherous had pulled out. The shook bikers were pulling shit out their ass. When Treacherous told them to put their guns in the bag too, I couldn't believe my ears.

"We ain't packin'. He the only one dat was strapped, cuz," one of the bikers volunteered, referring to the one Treacherous had made an example of.

Here it was these jokers was out here in VA trying to get their ball on knowing we played the murder game in Virginia, especially in Richmond, when it came to anybody who came from out of state, and only one of them traveled with a burner between the six of them. I had to laugh at that one.

"Y'all some dumb asses," Treacherous spit as he pulled out his Rambo knife. Eyes widened at the sight of it. One by one, he plunged the knife into the front and back tires of each bike. We then backpedaled to our own bikes. Before we pulled off, Treacherous shot each biker in the kneecap. "Next time bring backup," he clowned the injured bikers and then we were off and in the wind. It always turned me on to see my man in action just as I know it did the same with him whenever I got gangstress with it. As we darted up Chamberlain and then onto I-95 North, twenty minutes up the interstate, Treacherous signaled for me to pull off onto the exit. When we reached the intersection and he lifted up his helmet, I was not surprised by the words that came out his mouth.

"Babe, that shit got my dick hard as hell the way we just took them Bamas."

"I know. My shit was creamin' watchin' you handle them clowns," was my response I knew it turned him on even more when I talked dirtier and just as rough as him. "We gotta do something," he said. I knew what was coming next. We rode for another fifteen minutes through town before we found an open field. I followed as Treacherous did a hundred and twenty miles per hour through the open land. Once he had come to a complete stop, he was off his bike and tossing *his helmet before I was able to fully park mine. He approached and prevented me from exiting my bike.*

"Nah stay right there," he ordered. I took off my helmet and tossed it near his. He leaned in to kiss me, and I wrapped my arms around his neck and passionately returned it. He reached down and unfastened my black Seven jeans, then I snaked my legs around him to make it easier for him. He reached back and snatched off one of my riding boots and slid my left leg out while holding me up in mid-air, then did the same with the right. He sat me back on my bike. I hurried and unbuckled his belt and pushed both his jeans and boxer briefs down to his thighs. I looked down and saw his rock-hard dick pulsating. Instantly my inner thighs moistened.

He hiked me up and slid his hardness inside my wetness. I arched my back and embraced him, all of him. He held me by the waist and bent my back over the seat of my bike. His strength enabled him to sex me in mid-air, having my back barely touching the seat. His thrusts were hard and deep. I know he was totally turned on when he sexed me like this and I enjoyed it. With each thrust my inner walls creamed. When his pace increased and his strokes became rabbitlike, I knew my sex muscles had gotten the best of him. He sprayed me inside with his love juices until he had no more left. He was winded and I was pleased—pleased I had satisfied my man and he had satisfied me.

"I love the fuck outta you," he said still trying to gain control of his breathing.

"You better," I replied. Afterward, we made it back to Norfolk in record-breaking time. When we got home we were both surprised to see that each bankroll the Texas bikers had tossed in the knapsack was full of hundred-dollar bulk, no less than ten stacks each. That night we had come off with seventy gees, not including the jewels.

Teflon closed her notepad and returned it to her locker. Her sex was throbbing as well as wet. She could feel her inner thighs dampening as she relived one of her and Treacherous' capers and heated sexcapades. She locked her locker and made her way to the bathroom. There, she pleasured herself to images of Treacherous. Once she brought herself to an orgasm, she showered again and responded to Rich's letter before calling it a night.

CHAPTER FOUR

"The library will be closing in ten minutes. Please return all typewriters," the law librarian announced.

Rich took his ribbon out of the typewriter and unplugged it. He then packed up his belongings, turned the typewriter in and made his way back to his housing unit. During his seven-minute walk from the library to his unit, Rich was greeted with respect by his peers, young and old alike. Rich felt the amount of respect he had in the facility a gift and also a curse. He embraced the love and respect shown throughout his incarceration, but some he could have done without. Nearly five years ago when they televised his son's and his girlfriend's last moments of freedom and announced his own past street activities, every wannabe and up-and-coming thug or gangsta wanted to befriend him, hoping to find out what he knew. It was the type of attention Rich didn't particularly care for. Even some of the old-school gangstas and bank robbers invited him to join them in their reminiscing sessions of their heydays. Each time, he respectfully declined. The ones from the streets who intended to return to them, respected those who had put work in them and played the game to the fullest. Rich knew he was viewed as one of those individuals.

After twenty-two years, Rich had seen the game change ten times over, just from the breed and caliber of inmates who came and left behind the walls that had been his residence. Through that experience, he became all the wiser and knew he wanted no part of the new generation that ran the streets, knowing he'd get an express one-way ticket right back into the penal system once he got out. After all, prison hadn't broken or scared him. It only made him smarter and more cautious. Two things he knew would keep him out in the real world. Rich reached his unit and made his way to the dayroom.

"They already called you O.G. Here you go," Rich's cell mate said, handing him his mail. He was the only one Rich allowed to get his mail. Rich went into one of the unit's quiet rooms to read the letter he had just received from Teflon.

I hope this letter finds you in the best of health and spirits by the time it reaches your presence. As always, it was good hearing from you. You know that without the comforting and motivational words in your letters, I would not have lasted this long. Glad you're enjoying the chapters I've been sending you. Like before, you're going to have to wait until I write the next couple of chapters because the ones I have now are the intimate parts of the book. Like I told you, I don't need you all up in me and your son's personal business (smile!), but I got you, father-in-law.

Still no news on Little Treach. I count the days down that you're released and hope you are able to locate him like you said you would. One of us has to find him and guide him before it's too late. Where your time is limited, mine has really just begun, so there's nothing I can do for him from in here. It's up to you to save your grandson. You know 'the life' in his blood so I can only imagine how he will be ten, fifteen, or twenty years from now. If he's anything like the three of us, he may not even make it that far. It's because of my mother I survived as a child. It's because of your son I survived as a woman. It's because of my child I chose to live. It is because of you that I continue to fight, and it is because of me that I'm still here. This is all I know, and this is all I've ever had. Two are gone, and three of us are still here. Let's cherish and protect that at all costs. We're in this together, now. I look forward to hearing about your union with your grandchild and the restoration of your freedom.

Eternal and Bullet Proof Love.

Always Your Daughter-in-law aka Your Ride Or Die Chick

Rich folded the letter and returned it to the envelope. Teflon's letters always touched him in the deepest way. Her words were always so powerful to him. She reminded him so much of Treacherous' mother, Teresa. He could see why his son had loved her so much. From reading the chapters Teflon had been sending him about her and his son's life as a team, he couldn't help but compare them to him and Teresa. He realized Treacherous was like him in so many ways, especially after reading the last few chapters Teflon recently sent him. Prior to reading the pages detailing his son's life, Rich had no clue Treacherous had acquired a passion and love for motorcycles just as he had. He also hadn't known that Treacherous had inherited his enthusiasm and drive for robbing banks. One caper he read about reminded him of a stickup he had committed while Treacherous' mother was with him. Rich chuckled to himself as he briefly reminisced.

"Rich, where are you going?" Teresa had asked, coming out of the bathroom wearing only her sheer black nightgown. Rich had just checked his two revolvers and slipped on his burgundy leather blazer.

"Steppin' out for a minute. I'll be back shortly," he replied. He purposely avoided eye contact with her and kept his back turned. He knew with just one look she would see right through his words.

"I thought you were going to take off this weekend, baby," she reminded him.

Rich had contemplated making up something but knew it would be pointless, especially when Teresa already was suspicious of where he was headed and what he intended to do. "I'm bored. I'm just gonna shoot over to the juke joint in Newport News and see if anything's happenin' on that end of town. That was Rich's way of saying he was going to see if someone was out worth robbing "I'm going with you, then," Teresa had announced, already slipping into a pair of jeans and throwing on a tube top.

"Momma, I'm taking the bike," Rich shot back. He knew how much Teresa hated riding on the back of his Kawasaki.

"I don't care. I'm still going." Rich knew it was useless to argue with her once her mind was made up. He shook his head, snatched up his helmet, and made his way to the front door.

"And I'll go in to see if anything is happenin' tonight. If it is, then I'll bring them out and you stay can outside," Teresa had told him, snatching up the other helmet. Again, Rich said nothing, but smiled to himself. Richie Gunz lurked in the darkness on his pearl machine awaiting Teresa's exit out of the Newport News saloon. He checked his watch for the fifth time. Teresa had been in the bar for more than an hour. He was not the least bit worried, but anxious. He knew if she had stayed in the establishment that long then she had locked in on a potential jook. The door of the juke joint flew open and Rich saw Teresa exiting the bar holding up a six foot four, slightly staggering light-skinned brother with wavy hair, a butterfly collared paisley shirt, blue jeans too tight for Richie's taste and brown cowboy boots. Rich noticed he had stumbled out the door and nearly lost his balance, but what caught his eye the most was the man's hand constantly sliding down on Teresa's ass. Richie's blood boiled like a pot of hot grits on high.

As if Teresa could read Rich's mind, she put her hand up for only him to see and signaled for him to remain at bay. Rich laughed because he had already drawn his turns and was about to swarm down on the john. Rich watched as Teresa escorted the man to his assumed vehicle. Rich's demeanor changed when he saw where Teresa and the man had stopped. Rich wasted no time making his way over to where they stood.

"Beautiful, I told you I got it. I'm good," the tall light-skinned brother slurred. "Let me ride me to my place." He laughed at his own joke, reaching for the Harley Davidson keys Teresa had taken out of his hands.

"No, big boy, you've had one too many. I got this," she said. "I don't wanna die before I get to enjoy you," she added seductively. Teresa could see the lust tap dancing in the tall light-skinned brother's eyes as he took in her words.

"That sounds good to me, sweetness. I stay out in Virginia Beach on the beach front. Can you get me there?"

"No problem, honey," Teresa answered, hopping on to the Harley. The tall light-skinned brother was admiring the way Teresa's ass spread on the seat of his machine. Rich could only imagine the things running through the john's head the way he stood back eyeing Teresa. Just as he raised his left leg, he was knocked off balance by a sudden blow to the side of the head. Instantly he went tumbling down, crashing onto the pavement. He never knew what hit him. That is until he looked up and saw Rich towering over him.

"Hey, man, what's your problem?" the light-skinned brother snapped.

"You, you pretty muthatfucka!" Rich barked, shoving one of his twin revolvers in the victim's face.

"What I do?" he asked innocently.

"Shut the fuck up," Rich ordered. "Baby, hold this. He move, you know what to do." The light-skinned brother saw that Rich was talking to the pretty sister with the big butt he was probably hoping to get lucky with later.

"Ain't this about a bitch, you stankin' ass..."

He never got to finish his sentence. "Lights out, nigga." Rich had brought the butt of his gun crashing down on the light-skinned brother's temple. He had relieved him of the four gold chains and medallion, his nugget watch, and three link bracelets, along with a wad of cash he later found out totaled thirty-five hundred dollars.

"Baby, follow me on my bike," Rich had instructed Teresa. He handed her his keys and hopped on the Harley. Rich drove until he reached Chesapeake Park. As much as he liked the experience hog, he knew he couldn't keep it. Besides, it wasn't about the motorcycle, Rich wanted to make a statement. He knew how bike owners felt about their machines. He wanted to disrespect something he knew the light-skinned man loved just as he disrespected someone Rich loved. Teresa watched as Rich unloaded both of his revolvers into the Harley Davidson. She knew the reason behind destroying the bike. It was times like this that made her love him the way she did. That night they made love until they exhausted themselves and fell asleep.

Rich snapped out of his trance hearing the officer's thunderous voice call count. He made his way to his assigned area to prepare for count time, anticipating it to clear so he could write Teflon back.

CHAPTER FIVE

Teflon's stopwatch beeped indicating she had completed her two-mile jog around the facility's track. She walked an additional two laps to cool her body as she took in the sounds of Akinelli's throwback cut "I Need a Gangsta Bitch" on her Walkman. As she walked, she noticed a short, petite, char-coal-complected female staring at her the first time she passed by. The girl seemed vaguely familiar, but she couldn't quite figure why. She knew it wasn't from the compound because she made it her business to lock in any and all faces to be on the safe side, due to all the dirt she and Treacherous had done on the streets.

This girl's face was a new one in the woman's prison. Teflon actually remembered when the girl came in six weeks ago. Thinking back, she was almost certain the little girl had ice-grilled her for a split second, seeing the familiar look on her face. Rather than speculate or wait, Teflon approached the girl. Teflon's sudden movement caught the girl off guard. Teflon saw her entire expression went from hard core to marshmallow. That caused Teflon to downplay the situation.

"Where do I know you from?" Teflon asked, pulling the earphones off. "Probably from Norfolk. I'm from Tidewater," the girl replied. Hearing where the girl was from put Teflon on point, though the girl didn't seem like

too much of a threat. Treacherous was from Tidewater, and she remembered how he had terrorized the area. Besides, Teflon was not the type to
have female friends or any friends for that matter. In their line of work, both
she and Treacherous kept their circles very small and even tighter.

"Why would you think I know you from there?" Teflon questioned,
watching the girl carefully.

"You're Teflon, right?"

"Yeah and?"

"Well, I know you ride bikes and I ride, too. I remembered seeing you
out there at the Afram Fest some years back," she calmly confessed. Teflon
saw right through the front. She knew the last time she had visited the
Historical Afram Festival and why, but still she couldn't figure out where
the girl fit into the equation. For the life of her, she couldn't place her
anywhere at the festival. She was normally good with faces, but this one
wasn't registering. Nontheless, she grew tired of the back-and-forth and
decided to put an end to it.

"You didn't see me at the fuckin' Afram and you damn sure don't know
me, so what the fuck's your problem?"

"You bitch!" the girl roared just as she slipped a jailhouse-made knife
from under the sleeve of her sweatshirt and launched an attack against
Teflon. Her slowness and inexperience caused her to fail in the attempt and
allowed Teflon to capitalize off it. Teflon sidestepped the girl and faded like
The Matrix. The girl spun back around as quickly as she could, only to be
met with the razor blade Teflon had spit out of her mouth. Out of nowhere
she slashed the five-foot girl across the forehead. The girl went down from
the blow, clasping her forehead with both hands. Teflon was tempted to
continue her attack but was not in the mood to be forced to go to solitary
confinement. Instead, she inconspicuously trotted off, leaving the girl rolling
in her own blood.

Teflon had already showered and re-dressed by the time the code on
the compound was called. The place was locked down, and everyone was
instructed to report to their assigned housing. A full body search was con-
ducted on all females in the facility, but to no avail. Teflon was surprised and
respected the fact the girl hadn't snitched. Because she hadn't told who

committed the assault on her, the girl was taken into protective custody. Later word got out that she was the baby's mother of an ex-baller from New Jersey by the name of Brickz. He was murdered during Afram weekend after leaving with some biker chick from Club Reign.

Teflon remembered the incident all too well and was not mad at the girl for trying to ride out for her child's father. There was no doubt in her mind if she had been in those shoes she would have done the same only she would have been successful in her revenge, she realized confidently. Apparently the girl hadn't done her homework, Teflon thought. It was evident to her the girl had no clue or way of knowing she had tried to ride on a chick not to be fucked with.

Teflon laughed to herself. She couldn't wait to write Rich and tell him and made a mental note to include the incident in her memoir.

CHAPTER SIX

"You have a prepaid call from a federal correctional facility. To refuse this call, please hang up. To accept this call, dial five now."

Rich could hear the painful cough coming through the phone before he was able to speak a word. He waited until his only friend was done.

"What the hell took you so long?" O.G. complained as the cough faded. Rich was also his only friend.

"You know I don't like talking on these people's phone," Rich replied. "I'm just checking in, that's all."

"If that's why you called then you could've saved your money 'cause everything's smooth sailing on this end," O.G. shot back.

Rich smiled. For as long as he could remember O.G. had always been like that, having a never let 'em see you sweat type of attitude. He and O.G. had known each other for more than forty years, long enough for Rich to know O.G. was short for Orlando Goines and not just Original Gangster like everyone in the streets assumed. Being twelve years Rich's senior, O.G. was not only his friend but also was like a father figure to him. It was O.G. who had actually showed him the ropes on the streets when he had taken them on full time. Outside of his mother, only O.G. knew what he had done to his father. It was with O.G. he committed his first murder. It was O.G.

who schooled him on raising Treacherous in the absence of Teresa, and it was O.G. who had been doing jail time with him since he was charged with bank robbery. The two of them had an extensive history together.

"This is me you talking to, Orlando," Rich addressed O.G.

"Sucka, if I could get through this phone I'd kick yo' ass for callin' me that jive ass name," O.G. spat through coughs.

"You'd probably pass out before you get to me." Rich chuckled.

"You probably right." O.G. returned the laugh.

"Seriously, friend, talk to me. What did the doc say?" Rich's tempo changed.

O.G. let out a deep sigh. "That cracker don't know what the hell he's talking about."

Whenever he tried to downplay a situation, Rich knew it was something serious, but he didn't want to push his friend.

"They never do when it comes to us, but what did he say?"

"That's just it. The muthafucka didn't say nuthin'—not shit I wanted to hear anyway."

Getting something out of O.G. was like pulling teeth, Rich knew. His beating around the bush furthermore let Rich know it was more serious then he imagined. To him, O.G. was the one person he thought would outlive, despite their age disparity. To think that would not be the case was unimaginable for Rich, but he realized it might very well be the reality. Either way Rich wanted to know.

"What did the cocksucker say?" Rich tried a different approach on his friend.

"That white-faced nigga gonna tell me there's nuthin' they can do for me. I started to shove my pistol in his goddamn mouth and tell 'im to check that shit again but I played it cool and told him to kiss my black ass and left."

Although it was no laughing matter, Rich couldn't help but let out a slight chuckle imagining his friend's reaction to the doctor's words even though he sympathized with O.G.

"How the hell is he gonna say that when I know cases of colon cancer where niggas done got treated and still kickin'?"

There was a brief pause. "It ain't just colon cancer no more, Gunz," O.G. stated.

"He said I took too long and the shit spread. I didn't wanna tell you 'cause you didn't need this shit on your mental, but you all I got, and you deserve to know. I'm fucked up out here, baby boy. My whole right side locked up on me. I told the doc to give it to me raw with no chaser, and he said it's just a matter of time before this ragged-ass disease starts eatin' at my brain."

"Damn O.G.," was the only thing Rich could muster up. He felt as if someone had just plunged a knife into his heart. After thirty years, to think about walking out of this place and not being able to see the one person who rode with him day for day bothered Rich. For the first time in his life, Rich felt completely alone. In just a few more years he would be a free man, and he now realized that he had no one to go home to. He started going down the list in his head of those he lost in life. Before prison there was his one true love, Teresa. While staying in prison, there was his son, Treacherous. Now, O.G. Rich's mind began to drift. His thoughts began to take him back to the last time he had seen Teresa before she died giving birth to his son. Images of her on the operating table hemorrhaging invaded his mind. His thoughts then flashed to the day he stood in the dayroom of the federal facility and watched on television as his son chose his final fate by holding court on the interstate. Rich revisited the eventful day he'd been carrying with him since that happened.

"We now bring you live footage from Julie Sanchez of the actual chase. Hey, Julie, what do you have for us?"

"Hello, Bob. As you can see, police are in a massive pursuit of a brand-new all black 600 CLS Mercedes Benz. Suspects are believed to be armed and dangerous. So far, all we know is that suspects entered onto Highway 264 westbound, coming off the ramp, headed toward the Virginia Beach area. It has been confirmed, Bob, that there are two occupants inside the vehicle, both African American—one male, the other female. Our sources who have been following the incident since it erupted, tell us that the driver has been identified as thirty-year-old Treacherous Freeman from the Tidewater Park area in Norfolk, and thirty-year-old Teflon Jackson from the Georgetown section of Chesapeake. Sources also say Ms. Jackson may have been injured at the actual scene. Though the actual count has not been confirmed, we are told that Mr. Freeman allegedly shot and possibly killed several officers and pedestrians during the horrendous gun battle, fleeing the scene of the crime while many others were wounded.

"The emergency medical team is tending to those who were fortunate enough to have survived this unbelievable tragedy. As far as we know, no one was injured inside. Both Mr. Freeman and Ms. Jackson have past criminal histories. Police authorities continue to pursue the two suspects who seem as if they have no intention of giving up at this time. We'll keep you updated as this tragic story continues to unfold here on Highway 264. This is Julie Sanchez, live from WAVY 10. Back to you, Bob."

"Thanks, Julie. Keep us posted. In other news, two teens were gunned down in the parking lot of a local McDonald's on Princess Ann Boulevard. Hold on- this just came in. Our sources have found out that the black Mercedes Benz CLS that police had been in pursuit of just hours ago was reported stolen earlier today. It has now been confirmed that the CLS 600 Mercedes belonged to a Marcus Bullock of Brooklyn, New York. Mr. Bullock and another teen were gunned down in front of a local McDonald's on Princess Ann Boulevard after being car jacked by Mr. Freeman and Ms. Jackson. The local authorities have confirmed the connection between the McDonald's murders and the bank robbery. Our sources also tell us that Mr. Freeman's father, a Mr. Richard Robinson, was convicted more than seventeen years ago for single-handedly robbing the same bank for more than a million dollars. He is currently serving a thirty-year sentence in Petersburg Federal Institution."

Everyone in the dayroom turned and looked at Rich who continued watching TV.

"Although this hasn't been confirmed, it is believed to be true that Mr. Freeman and Ms. Jackson took close to two million dollars. Hold on, I've just been told there has been some new developments in our top story. Julie, are you there?"

"Yes, Bob, as you can see the pursuit has come to an end. Police have the entire highway shut down. After reaching the Virginia Beach exit, the SUV stopped on the ramp. Our sources tell us that Mr. Freeman and Ms. Jackson were ordered to throw out their weapons along with the vehicle keys, and they complied. We've also been told that the officer in charge instructed the occupants to exit the vehicle. Apparently this is what authorities are waiting for to take the suspects into custody. Hold on. The driver door just opened. Oh my god! As you can see, one of the suspects has opened fire on the authorities. It appears to be Mr. Freeman who is the actual gunman. There has been no sign of Ms. Jackson, but Mr. Freeman continues to attack authorities, as they are under rapid fire. I can't believe this is actually happening. For those of you who have just tuned in, this is live coverage of the shootout between one of the alleged bank robbers of Bank of America and the authorities. Wait! Something seems to be happening. Police are running toward the Mercedes."

Rich had watched as his son was gunned down on live television. He hadn't shed a tear up until that moment since the last time he visited with his son. As he continued to listen to the anchorman, his face moistened.

"It's been confirmed that this disastrous incident has ended in tragedy. Six state police and four federal agents were killed in the line of duty, five others were wounded. Mr. Treacherous Freeman was shot and killed during the horrendous shoot out. Miraculously, Ms. Teflon Jackson was found unconscious inside the vehicle with a bullet-inflicted wound, but our sources say she is not expected to make it. The money was recovered inside the Mercedes. What drove a young man to such a tragic ending, no one knows but that man himself. This is Julie Sanchez, live from WAVY TV 10."

"You have one minute remaining," was what snapped Rich out of his trip down memory lane.

"O.G., it's almost count time. I'ma call you back after it clears."

"Don't bother, Gunz. I sent you some things in the mail. You should get 'em tomorrow or the next day. Call me then and we'll discuss everything."

"Fair enough," Rich answered, respecting his wishes. The phone cut off before he could get to ask O.G. what he had sent him. He was tempted to call back after the prison head count cleared to find out but decided against it. Something in the way O.G. had informed him of the mail he intended to receive just didn't sit right with Rich. As he walked to his area Rich wondered what it could be he was expecting.

CHAPTER SEVEN

It was two in the morning and Teflon could not sleep. She had been tossing and turning all night. It was March 3. For many people, that day was just an ordinary one, but to Teflon it was more than that. It was Treacherous' birthday, and she could not stop thinking about him, which was nothing new, but this day was different. It was this date that made it possible for the two of them to ever meet. Images of him and her invaded her sleep. As usual whenever she thought of Treacherous, Teflon pulled out her pen and pad from underneath her mattress and turned on her nightlight. She had intended to start on the chapter she had in mind sometime throughout the course of the day but decided now was as good a time as any. She opened the spiral notepad and began to put her thoughts down on paper.

She named the chapter Memorial Weekend.

The entire week leading up to Memorial Day Weekend was an unforgettable one for me and Treacherous. A lot was going on. This was the first time the two of us had actually utilized assistance outside of ourselves. Although everyone within the seven cities knew how we got down, no one ever knew our business, but it was Treacherous' decision, and I rode with him on his call. I knew it took a lot for him to ask for help or accept it, so if he agreed to it then he had definitely thought it through thoroughly.

"Treach, did that call come through yet?" I asked.

"Not yet, boo. Still waitin' on this joker. If he don't reach out to me by tomorrow then I'm gonna hit him 'cause I don't wanna blow this opportunity down Bike Week. I'd rather have something definite set up versus us freestylin' trynna find a lick."

The joker Treacherous was referring to was a guy named Pete who was originally from New Jersey but got into some trouble when he was a juvenile and ended up in the Norfolk Detention Center. He normally despised northerners but said Pete was an exception to the rule because he had strong southern ties. His family migrated from South Carolina and Virginia to the north, but a great deal of them still lived in the south, which kept him coming down to visit.

Treacherous said I knew him from when we were in the detention center. Up until now there was only one nigga I had eyes for or even paid attention to. No one else was important to me, and he knew it. Treacherous had told me that out of all of the fights throughout the years he had served in the youth facility, Pete was the only one who had given him a run for his money. It was because of that, Treacherous said, he befriended him when the two had run into each other at Myrtle Beach a couple of years back. Treacherous had told me that Pete had relocated to South Carolina after he left the detention center and started getting money out there, but occasionally dabbled in our line of work. No matter what the case was, if Treacherous trusted him, then so did I.

"Whatever you say, I'm with you, babe," I agreed.

"Yeah, that's the best route, and just so you know, we're not gonna ride our bikes down to South Carolina. Just to be on the safe side, rather then ride three to four hours down and risk tippin' somebody off who might be going down from this way, we might as well get a truck cover 'em up and pull 'em."

"Okay," I stated. "That makes sense. And you don't even have to tell me that the truck we gonna get to pull 'em will leave from VA but won't make it back." I could always finish Treacherous' next thought.

We were just that close.

"You know it, boo."

As we cruised the local area in Treacherous' Yukon I noticed a familiar face.

"Babe, look right there." I pointed.

"Where?"

"Right there, ole boy, the tall light-skinned one with the blue Yankee fitted on."

"Who the fuck is that?"

"That's the clown-ass nigga I told you that said that slick shit to me when we were down by Military Circle mall the other day."

Treacherous took a closer look. "Nah you ain't tell me that and that nigga still walkin' around breathin'," Treacherous spit.

I couldn't help but smile at how overprotective he was when it came to me.

"No, babe, it wasn't like that. I already know his life was spared. Remember when I came back and told you some bozo tried to push up on me when I was coming from the bathroom but we were pressed for time because we were scoping out ole boy and his man from Bad News?" I refreshed his memory.

"That nigga?" He pointed in disbelief.

"Yup."

"Hold up, as a matter of fact, I think he was up in da club The Alley when we were squattin' on them jokers, too, or either Blakely's out in Chesapeake, one of 'em," Treacherous recalled.

"Maybe, I don't know, but I knew we'd see him again," I said.

"We about to see him right now," Treacherous barked, attempting to pull over.

"No, babe, keep going," I instructed.

"What?"

"Nigga, you heard me. I said keep going."

Just as I would never question him, Treacherous did not question me either. Instead he waited until I provided him with an explanation.

"Guess what that nigga drives, babe?" I asked.

"Come on with the guessin' games," he replied semi-heated that I didn't let him get out and take the light-skinned kid's life.

"Babe, just guess."

"A tricycle."

"No, Steve Harvey. A Harley truck," I boasted.

Instantly Treacherous' mean mug was replaced with a smile. He knew I was letting him know this was our means of transportation to South Carolina.

"And that shit is gonna leave VA but it won't be comin' back, just like his ass," Treacherous stated.

"I knew you were gonna say that."

"We gotta find out where this nigga lay his head at."

"On it. Been on it," I told him.

"What did you find out?"

"The next day I saw him talkin' to Gov when I went to go get us some pizza."

"Who? The Ghetto Governor?" Treacherous said, using his full street monarch.

"Yeah."

"Okay. What happened?"

I started to get his punk ass then but it was too many people around, so I let it ride, and that's when I saw him hop in the Harley truck. Gov went up in Domino's and I followed. As soon as he saw me he spoke and asked about you. I told him you were lying low, as usual. I think he thought I was trynna get 'em by the look on his face when he first saw me. You know Gov get that money, too—that legal money. I put him at ease though and gave him a hug.

"Yeah, Gov should know he one of the ones we fuck with," Treacherous interjected.

"Especially since he's always hookin' us up with the free passes to all the major events in the city- but then what, though?"

"After we ordered I asked Gov who ole boy was. At first he acted like he had amnesia until I described the dude. The first thing came out his mouth about ole boy was 'Don't tell me that nut-ass nigga said

something fly out of his face to you. If he did, he must didn't know who you was.'"

I downplayed the situation but Gov knew. He told me he was one of them dope boys from North Carolina and be traveling back and forth between here, ATL, and SC moving weight. He said when he's in town he's usually driving the silver Harley Davidson truck with the twenty-sixes on it and got a spot down in Hampton off the Boulevard. He didn't have an address for me, but he said he stays in a white house with a double-door garage and it be helluv bikes in the front yard and a few pit bulls in some kennels on the side of the house. He also told me the kid works alone, doesn't have a crew out here with him. Always brags about how much work he put in and will put in if someone thinks it's sweet. Gov said every time he runs into the nigga he got a different piece of hardware on him. By the time he finished telling me all of that his pizza was ready. I offered to pay him for the love but he refused. He wouldn't even let me treat him to his pizza, so I told him we owed him one and he knew how to get at us if he ever had a problem. Before we parted, he asked if we were goin' to Myrtle for Bike Week. I thought he was gonna say he had a problem down there but he just wanted to know because he thinks we got the best bikes in the world. He said he was going so I made a mental note of that and didn't give him a definite answer as to whether we were. What I actually told him was we were thinking about shooting down to Miami. It's not that I don't trust him but the less he knew the better."

"That's what's up. You did right," Treacherous said when I finished. "Yeah, we owe Gov one for that though."

Once we mapped out how we were going to run down on the North Carolina hustler, Treacherous and I sexed and took it down for the night.

The next morning I woke Treacherous to the smell of turkey sausages, scrambled eggs with cheese, home fries, and buttered and jellied toast with a tall glass of orange juice.

"Babe, get up." I shook him.

He was dead to the world, and I knew the reason why.

"Babe, get up," I repeated. *"I made us some breakfast."*

"What time is it?" he asked in the raspy tone I so loved, rolling over. It was in the morning when his voice was most harsh. Something about it just sent chills through my body.

"It's seven-thirty."

"Seven-thirty," he growled. When he opened his eyes he saw me standing there in my lucky powder-blue Victoria's Secret matching bra and thong set holding his breakfast in hand.

"Yeah, seven-thirty, nigga. The same time we always get up," I shot back. *"I knew I wore that ass out. You couldn't hang with the Teflon Don. I put that hardcore gangster lovin' on that muthfuckin' ass last night. Lil Kim ain't got shit on me. Who's the baddest bitch?"* I teased.

"I'mma let you get that," Treach said with his signature smile, *"and because you poppin' shit, after we make this next move I'mma tear that ass up."*

"Whatever," was all I said.

"You know how I get after a good hit."

And he was right. Just the thought of us knocking off the light-skinned hustler from North Carolina made my inner thighs moisten. The best sex Treacherous and I ever had was after committing a robbery. In fact, all of our best sex encounters were after one of our capers.

"Thanks for breakfast, boo. I was starving."

"You're welcome, babe. Now hurry up and scarf that down. I already showered and I left it running for you."

"Did you get anymore soap?" he asked, shoving an entire turkey sausage into his mouth.

"Yes I got you some more Lever Cool Fresh liquid soap," I answered, knowing that's what he was really asking. That was his favorite and the only kind he'd use since it came out.

"That's why I love you, Tef."

"I love you, too. Now hurry up. By the time you're done in the shower I should be dressed. I already ironed your black V-neck tee and some black jeans, and I pulled out your black high-top Pradas."

"Thank you, baby." After eating one more forkful of eggs, Treach-erous hopped out of bed and into the shower. I just couldn't resist. I made my way into the bathroom, removed my bra and panties and put on my shower cap. The glass shower door was so steamed up and the water was running so hard he never noticed me. He was washing his face when I entered the shower. I wrapped my hand around his semi-erect dick making him aware of my presence.

"I thought you were supposed to be gettin' dressed." He shook his head.

"I was," I replied just as I slithered my way down between his legs. Without hesitation I took Treacherous into my mouth.

"Boo, go ahead. Why you starting?" He moaned. I paid him no mind. The water tap-danced on my back as I pushed him to the back of the shower, placed my hands on the side of his hips, and continued tasting my man.

"Sshit, boo, don't start nothing you know you can't finish." Treach-erous pushed me off him. With his hardness still in my mouth I looked up at him.

"I'm serious," he said.

I just smiled and got up. *"Punk,"* I said before exiting the shower.

"I needed that. That shit felt good," Treacherous said in reference to the shower walking into the room in the nude. The way his abs glistened and indented caused my heart to skip a beat.

"That's the only thing that felt good?" I continued to tease.

His silence told me he was done playing and was focusing on the upcoming business we had to handle. I immediately got into work mode.

"We gonna take the bikes today since we haven't rode 'em in a few days. We need to open 'em up and make sure they're good for Myrtle, anyway," he told me.

"That sounds good. Besides, it's riding weather out. The weather-man said it was going to be in the mid-eighties today."

Once we dressed, one after the other Treacherous and I pealed out on our bikes as they roared down the block. We jumped on 264 East headed out to Hampton. We weaved in and out of lanes and dipped in *and out of cars then made them bark all the way to the Hampton exit once we got some open road in front of us. The streets of Hampton were quiet when we came through. Treacherous and I glided through the town like two thieves in the night. Within minutes we were on the street The Ghetto Governor had told me the light-skinned kid from North Carolina lived on. Slowly we cruised down the block in search of the white house with the dog kennels on the side and the Harley truck parked out front. Treacherous covered the right side while I covered the left. After reaching the third intersection to no avail, Treacherous and I began to think we had been sent on a wild-goose chase. We didn't want to believe that Gov had given mis-information but that's what it looked like. My blood was simmering at the thought. I was actually looking forward to paying the light-skinned kid a visit. We were quickly approaching the end of the street. The closer we got, the more my blood boiled. I waved my hand to get Treacherous' attention then gestured that the info Gov had given was a dead end. He pointed just a few feet ahead. When I turned and looked, lo and behold, I saw the kennels full of pit bulls to my right. The infamous white house we were in search of was the last one on the block and sat caddy-corner. Treacherous and I rode to the end of the block and made U-turns.*

The dogs barked aggressively, rushing to the fence at the sight and sounds of our bikes. Just as Gov had said, we saw four bikes, but the light-skinned kid's Harley truck was nowhere to be found. I was disappointed because I had already envisioned shoving my nine down his throat and making him gag while he begged to have his life spared. We did a quick scan of the premises then rode off.

Once we were off the light-skinned kid's block Treacherous pulled over on the side of the road and lifted his helmet. "We got some time to kill. Whatchu wanna do?" he asked. He knew I was heated.

"I wanna ride around out here for a minute and see if we see that nigga truck before we go back home," I answered, letting my emotions get the best of me. That was not our style to ride around. We either planned or waited our licks out. My answer only confirmed to Treacherous that this was more than just another hit for me—it was personal.

"You sure?" he asked again, giving me the opportunity to get it together. That was one of the things I loved about him.

"Nah, let's get the fuck outta here," I replied.

"Don't worry, boo, we gonna get 'em. Trust me," Treacherous assured me.

"I know, babe."

"Come on, let's go get something to eat."

I nodded in agreement, pulled my helmet down, and followed my man's lead.

Twenty minutes later we were pulling in front of Treacherous' favorite Waffle House back in Norfolk.

"Ms. Janice, let me get two turkey patty melts and—"

"And make sure they clean the grill," she finished Treacherous' sentence. "Son, why do you always do that to Ms. Janice? Now you know I can never forget that. Hell you the only person I know been coming in here for over a year requesting that. Outside of the turkey melt, you only eat scrambled eggs and cheese on raisin bread, and turkey BLTs out of here," she said.

The two of us laughed to ourselves at Ms. Janice's rundown.

"I apologize," Treacherous offered.

"Um-hmm. What about you, sweetheart? What will you be having today?" She turned to me.

"I'll have a turkey BLT, please."

"Something to drink? Pepsi?" she offered, looking at Treacherous to further prove how well she knew his ordering habits.

We both smiled and nodded.

As we ate and went over our next moves, time escaped us. The morning had turned into the late afternoon by the time Treacherous and I finished eating and talking. Treacherous left Ms. Janice a healthy tip before we made our way out of the restaurant. Just as we were walking out the door the sound of Treacherous' ring tone "Keepin' It Gangsta" by Fabolous wailed off. He looked at the screen and gave me a nod, letting me know this was the call we had been waiting on.

"Yo," Treacherous answered, putting the phone on speaker so I *could hear. Although I loved to see him take charge in any situation and be so aggressive with everyone, I couldn't stand the way he answered the phone, especially when he answered "Yo", but I knew he wasn't a phone person so he kept his answers short. Besides he knew better than to "Yo" me.*

"What's good, my dude?" Pete greeted.

"You tell me," Treacherous replied.

"My bad for the delay. I got a little tied up, but everything's still everything on this end though. I got shit set up real sweet. I'm just putting the final touches on some things," was Pete's response.

"Dat's what's up. Say no more. We'll talk," Treacherous said, cutting him short. Even though he didn't say much what he had said was too much for Treacherous and for me. We never discussed business over the phone, let alone how we were going to conduct it.

"You in NJ or SC?" Treacherous asked, changing the subject.

"I'm back up top," Pete answered meaning New Jersey. "I'll be back in the dirty by the time the sun go down and comes back up though. I'll hit you when I'm in the area, and we can link up so we can chop it up more in depth. You know I can't come to VA, but we can meet in NC or something."

Treacherous had already told me how Pete had gotten on his feet by knocking off some dudes for a lot of product and even more money out in Portsmouth and hadn't been back in Virginia since except for passing through.

"Where in NC?"

"You know anywhere off I-95 is good for me," Pete told him.

"Where?" Treacherous repeated.

"How about we hook up off Exit 75 at the gas station. It's a club right there my man Big Tex own. That would be good for me anyway. I got a little honey that stays not too far from there in Dunn. I can stop off right quick and check her."

"I know the area. Just hit me," Treacherous agreed.

"Yup."

Treacherous hung up with not so much as a "peace" or "one" to end the call. He was rude like that even when he wasn't trying to be, but no one ever said anything—no one but me. This time I didn't. He knew I wanted to though, which is why he shot me that oh-so-loving smirk of his.

"Guess your boy is on point," I said instead.

"Seems like it."

"We'll see," I replied.

"Yeah, we'll see. But anyway, you remember that town Dunn he's talkin' about?"

I was waiting for him to ask me that. A few years back we had run through North Carolina on a massive robbing spree from Greensboro to Charlotte on down to Raleigh to Fayetteville. In our travels we had posted up in an area with a bunch of small surrounding towns like Smithfield, Benson, and Dunn in particular. At the time, out of towners getting money in the south were plentiful and we were coming across some nice licks of hustlers coming from up north down to the dirty. They were easy pickings. A few of them we actually had to leave alone because they wouldn't lie down without a fight. We had worked that area for about a month until some chicks from North Carolina blew the spot up by fumbling on a caper of a three-man team from New York that Treacherous and I had actually had our eyes on. I'd never forget that particular crew because it was the first time I had never gotten passed the name of any man I had ever gone after as a potential victim. I remember introducing myself to him at club Kamikaze in Raleigh and him telling me his name was Stacks right before he excused himself and never returned. The most we had found out about him and his two comrades was that one was his brother and the other his right-hand man. I saw him once more at club Taj Mahal when Biggie Smalls had performed, but he and his crew were accompanied by four women the rest of the evening. Weeks later we read in the local newspaper and heard on the news four female robbers and the head dude of the money-getting trio were found dead in a trailer out in the country. We immediately headed back to Virginia before any heat that didn't belong to us came our way.

"I remember," I grinned, reminiscing. *I knew what was coming next.*

"Not everybody is gonna fall head over heels for you at first sight, boo," he teased, remembering how the New York hustler Stacks didn't fall for my charm.

"Fuck you." I gave him the middle finger and hopped on my bike.

"Back at you." He returned the gesture and climbed on his bike too.

"Where to now?" I asked.

Treacherous glanced at his watch. Night fall was slowly approaching.

"Let's go check and see if that nigga made it back home."

His words were like music to my ears. *"Right behind you."*

As Treacherous and I cruised down the boulevard for the second time that day, the block was coming to an end. When we reached the last corner to cross over, my heart couldn't help but skip a beat. On the opposite side of the intersection there sat the silver Harley Davidson truck at the stop signing waiting to cross over. Treacherous and I both spotted the truck at the same time and busted a right at the corner rather than continuing straight. Once the truck crossed over we pulled over.

"Boo, don't worry. We're on his ass. It ends tonight," Treacherous said, turning his bike around.

I nodded and followed. We wasted no time catching up to the Harley truck, trailing at a nice distance, careful not to alarm him of our presence or the fact that he was being tailed. He was blasting music and the bass from his speakers was so loud, we were sure he couldn't hear us. Ten minutes later we pulled over and watched from afar as he parked in front of a local liquor store. Five minutes later he was back in his truck busting a U-turn in the middle of the street headed back in the direction where he lived. I hoped that was his final destination. We noticed he was so busy with his stereo system in the truck that he never even looked to his left. Had he done so it may have dawned on him that this was his second time seeing us that evening.

Since we knew where he laid his head we fell back and waited, *giving him enough time to get home.*

When we reached the top of the light-skinned kid's block we could see the Harley truck parked in the driveway. Treacherous lifted his helmet.

"You got your silencer on you?"

I felt the right arm of my leather jacket where I normally kept my silencers to my nine millimeter. "Yeah both of 'em."

"Let me get one so I can take care of the dogs. I forgot mine at home. You just go around the back and look for a way in."

"Okay, but what about the bikes?"

"We're gonna walk them and park them up in there." He pointed to the left, which was a dead end that faded into the woods. We killed the engines and cautiously walked our bikes into the hiding place Treacherous had chosen for us. With each house we passed we peered into windows from afar, looking to see if a nosy neighbor may have spotted us. Dressed in all black made it difficult for anyone to see us, but still we were alert.

Treacherous and I doubled back and made our way toward the light-skinned kid's house. The closer we got, the louder we heard the music blaring from inside.

Perfect, I thought as the pit bulls launched their barking assault, detecting our presence. All four dogs were silenced immediately with the shots Treacherous planted in their skulls. I heard each one's last cry as I moved pantherlike to the back of the house. Instinctively I checked the handle of the back door. There were times when it was that easy, but this time it wasn't. As I released the handle I caught a light go on causing me to fade to the side. Once I was away from the door and out of view I leaned in to see where the light had come from. I saw a tall caramel-complected female with what appeared to be a long frizzy blond weave down her back wearing nothing but a New York Jets jersey standing in front of the refrigerator. She danced to the sound of the music while she searched for what she was looking for. Once she retrieved it, she spun around and made her way to the cabinet. She was actually a pretty girl, kind of like a younger version of the singer

*Faith Evans. I could see that she had gotten a ginger ale and a cran-
berry juice. She reached on the top shelf of the cabinet, grabbed two
glasses, then made her way back to wherever she and the light-skinned
kid were apparently chilling.*

*"The muthafucka's not alone," I whispered to Treacherous, hear-
ing him walk up.*

*"Doesn't matter. They in the wrong place at the wrong time," he
shot back.*

I already knew what that meant.

*This time I lead and Treacherous followed. Treacherous knew when-
ever I took the lead I intended to control the situation and he had no
problem with that. There was no doubt in his mind that I was fully
capable of executing a plan just as good if not better then he could. In
no time I coasted through the kitchen and followed the sounds of the
music and the smell of an exotic weed in the air to the living room.
When I reached the doorway of the living room the first thing I saw
was the light-skinned kid stretched out on the plush couch puffing on
a blunt as the Faith Evans knockoff danced provocatively in front of
him with her glass in hand and a bottle of Remy sat in the ice bucket.
She took a sip of her drink and continued with her dance. With her
free hand she began to run her fingers through her blond weave. She
threw the rest her drink back, set the glass down, and attempted to
raise the Jets jersey over her head. That was my cue. Before she was
fully unclothed I was already behind the light-skinned kid. He had just
taken another pull of what smelled like Sour Diesel when he felt the
cold steel on his bald head.*

"What the—"

"Oh my god."

They both yelled in harmony over the music.

*I had my nine up against his dome and my forty cal pointed at
Faith Evans.*

*"Try some funny shit, nigga, and see if I don't open ya fuckin'
head up like a cantaloupe," I snarled. "Bitch, get ova there," I commanded with the wave of my other gun. In record-breaking time she
complied.*

"Yo, I ain't got shit, yo." He tried to sound tough.

I smacked him across the head with the nine.

"A yo-yo is a toy muthafucka. Now yo me again, and it'll be your last time yoing anybody else, pussy," I spat.

"A'ight, y—. Okay." He caught himself.

Just then Treacherous appeared. I knew he was in the background watching, enjoying me at work. Treacherous walked in front of the light-skinned kid as Faith Evans sat there in the nude shaking in fear. Treacherous picked up the jersey and tossed it to her. "Put that on," *he calmly instructed, never taking his eyes off the light-skinned kid. The girl acted as if she were in shock so I snapped her out of it.*

"Bitch, you heard what he said. Put that shit on before I wrap it around your muthafuckin' neck."

That was all the motivation she needed to slip the jersey over her head.

"Big man, what's this about?" the light-skinned kid asked Treacherous, holding the side of his head.

"Don't ask me, nigga. Ask her," Treacherous barked.

I could see the kid was tempted to turn around but thought better of it.

"Go ahead, muthafucka," Treacherous insisted.

Out of fear of what Treacherous would possibly do to him if he didn't comply, the light-skinned kid turned his head in my direction. I could tell by the way he tilted his head to the side that he was trying to place where he knew me from. Then as if it appeared out of thin air the widening of his eyes told me he had figured it out.

"Yeah, bitch." I launched a shot into his shoulder.

He screamed in agony, and for the second time Faith Evans sang with him.

"Shut the fuck up," Treacherous ordered the girl, pressing his glock up against her dome. Her screams instantly turned into silent cries.

"I'm sorry," he moaned, holding his shoulder.

"Sorry for what, nigga?" I wanted to hear him say it.

"For everything," he pleaded.

His arrogance cost him another shot. I dumped a round into the right leg.

"What the fuck is everything?" I questioned.

"Pleeaase!" he begged.

"I'ma ask you one more time," I warned, lining my nine up with his forehead.

He forgot all about his two wounds and threw his hands up to cover his face.

"For everything," he started. "Tryna push up, disrespecting you, even looking at you," he added.

I wanted to laugh at his last statement.

"Where that paper at?" Treacherous demanded, growing tired of the whole situation.

The light-skinned kid looked clueless.

"Muthafucka, you deaf?" Treacherous smacked him across the face with his hammer.

The impact of the blow caused some of the blood from his mouth to splash the sleeve of my leather jacket.

"It's upstairs in the closet in the shoeboxes," he managed to mumble. His mouth was bloodied, and I could see his lips beginning to swell.

"When I come back we out," Treacherous informed me. He didn't have to spell it out for me because I was already on it. As Treacherous went in search of the money, I got on my job.

"See what a big mouth gets you."

"I didn't mean—" were his last words before I silenced him with two rounds to his face.

I then walked over to Faith Evans who was now hysterical.

"Please don't kill me. I promise I won't say anything. I don't even know him. I just met him tonight."

"You should watch the company you keep," I told her before I pressed my forty cal up against her skull and pumped a round into it.

"This chump had the mother lode," Treacherous said, returning to the living room with two bags.

He scanned the room and saw I had taken care of my part. We exited quietly, the same way we had entered, and made it back to our bikes. Once we were out of the area, Treacherous doubled back and got the Harley truck. We loaded both bikes onto the back and drove to Norfolk safely. As promised, Treacherous sexed me gangster style until my body couldn't take it anymore. That night I came eight times to his none, and we came off with nearly ninety thousand in cash, a kilo and a half of coke, four pounds of weed and six guns.

The next day Treacherous and I decided to lay low. We hung around the house and watched gangster flicks. As usual we started with an oldie. Treacherous had chosen Hell Up in Harlem, Menace II Society, Hoodlum and Heat last time. It was my choice this time and I chose Black Cesar, Three The Hard Way, Set It Off and Durdy Game. We were three movies in when Treacherous' phone went off. He glanced at the screen.

"Yo, P, what's the deal?" he answered, placing the call on speaker. I paused the movie.

"Same shit, my dude," Pete replied.

"What's your status?" Treacherous wanted to know.

"I'm like a li'l over two hours away from where we gonna meet."

"That's what's up. Me and baby girl gonna jump on the road now, and we'll kick it then," Treacherous sat up and told him.

"Alright, my dude. See you when you touch."

Treacherous knew he didn't have to tell me anything. Although I was enjoying our quality time together I knew it was business time. I rolled out the bed and started getting dressed.

"Babe, you gettin' thicker," Treacherous complimented.

I just grinned and continued getting dressed.

"I'm for real." He put emphasis on his words, coming up behind me. He cuffed my ass cheeks with both hands and kissed me on my right collarbone.

"Didn't you just tell ya boy Pete you and baby girl are about to jump on the road?" I reminded him while fastening my bra from the front.

"He'll be there when we get there," was his response right before *he spun me around and persuaded my upper body to bend over the bed with a light push. I looked back at him and moaned, feeling his thick middle finger rub against my clit.*

"Damn you stay wet, babe." His tone grew deep.

"Only for you," I replied, reaching back for his rock-hard pole. I guided him inside me while he spread my ass cheeks. My muscles tensed as he penetrated my sex.

"Yeah, you got thicker." He moaned, sliding in and out of me.

His rhythm started out slow but with each thrust it increased.

"Yes, right there," I purred.

"Right there?"

"Yeah."

The head of Treacherous' dick brushed against my spot causing me to shudder. My inner muscles contracted around his hardness. He grabbed me by my waist, lifted my body midair and began pulling me into him. Whenever he did that I knew it was just a matter of time before he exploded. The heavy pounding caused me to climax for a third time. This time my pussy spasms were too much for him.

"Shit," he said right before his legs gave way under him. I could feel his juices showering my insides as he collapsed onto my back. I could feel his body slightly jerk and the head of his dick throbbing inside of me.

"Whose dick is this?" I asked him.

"Yours boo. Whose pussy is this?" he retorted.

"Yours," I replied seductively.

"It better be," he barked. I didn't even comment.

Knowing we were behind schedule, the two of us hopped in and out of the shower and hurried to get dressed. Within minutes we were dressed and out the door.

We had already loaded the bikes onto the Harley truck the previous night and packed our bags with all the necessities so we decided to post up on the outskirts near Myrtle Beach once we met up with Pete. We were nearly a half an hour away from Dunn, North Carolina, before Treacherous decided to pull off the exit.

"We need gas, and I'm starvin'."

"Me too." I rubbed my stomach.

Besides sharing the microwave popcorn during our movie time neither of us had eaten
all day.

Treacherous pulled up to the gas pump and we both hopped out.

"Babe, what do you want, Popeye's or Sbarro's?"

"Nah, I don't want no pizza. Get me two breasts and a wing with mashed potatoes. Let me get sixty on pump seven," he said all in one breath.

Within a few minutes, I was back to the truck with a three-piece meal for Treacherous and a two-piece meal for me. He was sitting in the truck parked to the side waiting for me.

"Pete called. He's already there," Treacherous announced as I hopped in.

"And?"

"And nothing. I'm just telling you. I told him we'd be there in under half."

Twenty-five minutes later we were veering off on Exit 75.

"There he go over there," Treacherous stated. Pete was leaning up against a gold Ford F-150 sipping on a bottled water. The truck was beautiful and had to have been the latest model.

From where we were he didn't look familiar. Even though Treacherous had said he had strong southern ties, Pete had northerner written all over him. He sported a fitted cap that came down low enough to conceal his eyes, a short-sleeved gray-and-black designer button-up shirt, which he wore open, revealing a long but semi-thin platinum chain with a medallion that draped down past his midsection. He had on a pair of charcoal-gray Capri cargo pants that were too long to be shorts due to his height and a pair of three-quarter gray with black G's Gucci shoes. We pulled alongside of him. Treacherous parked and got out. I witnessed the two of them exchange manly handshakes. At this time Treacherous noticed that I hadn't gotten out of the truck. He motioned for me to get out. Pete took off his fitted cap and wiped his *forehead of perspiration with a hand towel.*

"Long time, no see, Teflon," he greeted. I was hoping he didn't address me as "ma," "sweetheart," or any other title up-north cats used.

Not that it mattered, but now that he had his hat off he looked vaguely familiar. I may have recognized him more, but he bore a full razor-sharp beard that covered most of his face, and he was now built like the fighter Kimbo. His beard was like one Treacherous and I had seen most men sporting when we went to Philadelphia one year and offed some young money getters we had followed up there.

"Yeah, long time," I replied dryly.

"You don't remember me," Pete boldly stated. "How could you when you only had eyes for this brother right here?" He smiled, pointing to Treacherous. "That's what's up. Y'all two still together. I wish I could find something that strong."

Treacherous and I both nodded. I didn't like too many people, especially guys, but I liked Pete's style. He seemed down to earth and cool.

"I bet you I can tell you something you might remember," Pete said.

"What?" Treacherous said. I smiled on the inside. I knew he wasn't having that.

"Come on, my dude, you know I ain't gonna say nothing to get me and you to go another round, even though you owe me a rematch," he joked, referring to their last physical encounter in the youth detention center long ago.

"Any time," Treacherous said. His words could have been taken jokingly or seriously because his facial expression was blank but his tone was mild.

"I'ma remember that, but nah though. Teflon, you remember the girl from Diggs Park that used to bring you notes from Treacherous?"

I thought for a second. "Tammy?" I recalled

"Yeah. Do you remember after Treacherous left and you got off room lock and she showed you someone and told you she thought she found her Treacherous?"

I did remember. "Oh shit, that was you," *I replied.*

"Yup."

"She used to talk my ear off about you. I didn't wanna hear that shit, but that was my only associate, and she was loyal to me and Treacherous. Whatever happened to her?" *I really wanted to know.*

"She wrote me a few times when she got out, but then she stopped writing. You know I had juvenile life like big bro here, but at the time I was still fresh on my sentence. I think it was too much for her. One of the girls who was keepin' in touch with her put it out there that she got pushed over some dude she was messin' with from Richmond. I never tried to get the details."

"Really," *was all I said losing interest.*

"Yeah, that's what I said," *Pete said.*

"What's good with this Myrtle Beach joint?" *Treacherous got things back on track.*

"Oh, it's a go, my dude."

"So who are these jokers?" *Treacherous wanted to know.*

"They call themselves Fab-5 from T-Ville. That's a little small town called Timmonsville, Exit 157 off 95."

"So what's the Bike Week score lookin' like. I mean are they gettin' it or what?"

"Put it this way. They're called the Fab-5 'cause they're the five strongest dudes in the area. Their status down there is more on some rapper-celebrity-type shit. These cats own a couple of spots throughout South Carolina. You might've heard of some of them or cased a few of 'em out and just didn't know they were behind 'em. Club Spotlight in South Florence, 99 Degrees, and Hypnotic, both out west in Florence."

"Yeah, I'm familiar with all three."

"Well then you know these spots each pullin' in nothin' under twenty to thirty stacks three nights a week easy. I partied with these dudes outside of their spots and I never see' em with nothing under five stacks in their pockets. I went to Myrtle with them last year and they had nothing under ten apiece on 'em. On the low, these jokers usually be coppin' like five to ten birds at a time from me. That's how they really get their paper."

"So what type of dudes are they? They're just some roll-over types, or we gonna have a problem?" Treacherous asked the question I had been wondering.

"Nah, they're definitely not no pushover dudes. This the deal." He started his rundown. *"The one named Corey is the hotheaded one. He'll pop off at the drop of a dime. They call him Suicide 'cause when he's drinkin' he gets crazy. He pushed a nigga at a club over leaning against his Charger. Mark D is his right-hand man. He's the one you gotta watch 'cause he's kind of quiet, makes you think he doesn't want any problems but then later have the gun up in your mouth. Black is the fighter out the crew. He has no problem with buckin'. A few times he knocked a joker out who had a gun pointed at him. If he gets within reaching distance or feels his life is in jeopardy he won't hesitate to try you. Roton is Corey's cousin. He'll lay a joker out for any of his manz, but he'll lay his life on the line for Corey. Kev is the genius of the crew—college grad, computer wiz, chemist, and mastermind of their entire drug operation and legal businesses. He plays the background making sure the paper is flowing right, makes sure the product is right and comes up with the best way to handle beef if it comes their way. In some way or another they all are potential threats."*

"That means they all gotta get it then."

"I mean it's whatever," Pete said.

I listened as Treacherous and Pete discussed the upcoming caper. Based on what he had told Treacherous, I really wasn't moved by the numbers he was talking. Treacherous and I had taken risks for less, but we had never put together a job, especially so far away from home for the amount of money Pete was talking about.

"So you mean to tell me we doin' this job for a bout fifty grand or so? But not really once you get ya cut." I voiced my opinion on the matter. Judging by Treacherous' face I could tell we were on the same page with our thoughts.

"Absolutely not," Pete shot back. *"I was saving the best part for last. That's what took me so long to put it all together. I wanted to make sure this shit was worth it for all of us. While I was up top they hit me*

on the hip and placed their new order. Initially they wanted six bricks at first, but I convinced them they should up the order because my connect told me that it was about to be a drought and prices were about to go at least another four or five grand so they went up and ordered twelve, and the sweet part about it is they want me to bring it to where they're staying in Myrtle. They told me they're staying at The Anderson Resorts right there on Ocean Boulevard. Smell me?"

"Yeah. That's sweet right there," Treacherous replied.

"How much you charge them per key?" I wanted to know.

"Twenty-five."

I did a quick calculation in my head. "So that's three hundred grand?"

"Yup."

"Whatchu expectin' outta that?" Treacherous asked.

"Something light," Pete answered. "Just give me a hundred, and y'all keep the two."

That wasn't a bad deal at all, I thought, and neither did Treacherous.

"That's fair." Treacherous shook Pete's hand to seal the deal.

"I play fair, my dude," was Pete's comeback.

"Yo, so what type of heat you think these jokers gonna be packin'?" Treacherous asked.

"Really, not too much. Last year one of their peoples got bagged with the hammer on the way out there, and that kinda shook 'em to be travelin' like that with bud and liquor drinkin' and smokin' in the whip. They'll probably risk takin' about one with 'em but nothin' heavy. These dudes really about that paper rather then some gangster shit. I mean they'll do what they gotta do, but they don't go lookin' for trouble. Plus, they trust me, and they know I keep the heat at all times, and they know my gun go off. They got a lot of love and respect for me, and it was vice versa until my shortie down there told me how the dudes Corey and Mark D had been trynna get at her whenever I dip back up top and stay for a while. Dawg, if I was fucks with you I fucks with you, that means any and everything you claimin' is off limits, nah mean? It's not even about them comin' at shortie though. It's about how they went *about it," he clarified. "You know ain't nothing slow about me but my walk, my dude, so I didn't just take shortie word on face value without investigatin' the situation. I told her to slip both of them the number like she was interested, and if and when they call record the convo. I was buggin' off these dudes when I heard 'em trynna beat my back in just to try to smash. They was hittin' her with shit like they'd take care of her if she stopped fuckin' with me, how she'd never want for nothin', and how I'm not really their manz and that I'm not really from down there. They just do business with me and some more extra shit. But check this shit," he added, "I tell my shortie to dead one of them from callin' and pay more attention to the other. She deads Mark D and starts hollerin' at Corey heavy. I shoot down to ATL and NC and then stay up top so they think I'm doin' my normal. I tell her to feed the nigga some bullshit about how she ain't fuckin' with me no more and how she wish I'd just leave her alone and she wanted to be with him. This nigga fucks around and opens up to her about Myrtle Beach."*

"Whatchu mean?" Treacherous asked, not following but I had an idea.

"He tells her how they intend to set me up and off me for the birds and then he and her can live happily ever after. Smell me?"

"That's crazy." Treacherous laughed.

"Exactly. So ain't gonna be no happy endin' on this one, my dude."

"No doubt, but if that's the case then why you think they would only bring one gun if they know you comin' strapped?" Treacherous questioned.

"Because they think they got the drop on me, but you're right they could have more. No matter how many joints they got we gotta leave 'em stinkin' up in that piece."

"Definitely," Treacherous spit.

"No other way," I joined in.

"There it is then."

As usual Myrtle Beach was bike infested. Bike clubs, non-bike club riders, and wanna-be riders from all over flooded the city's streets. Females of all shapes, sizes, and colors rode shotgun on the back of some of the hottest bikes in the land while dudes performed tricks and stunts or just cruised. Some of the women were on the back of the bikes wearing g-strings and thongs while others chose miniskirts with nothing underneath as spectators snapped pictures and videotaped them with camcorders and cellular phones. The females who rode joined in the festivities of tricks and stunts as well. Some of them even sported other females on the back of their own bikes dressed similarly to the ones who rode on the back of dudes. If you were a true rider and had a love for bikes then this was the place you needed to be during Memorial weekend.

Treacherous and I cruised down Ocean Boulevard checking out the scene. As we approached Nineteenth Street, we noticed the sign that read The Anderson Resort. We locked the location in and continued to make our way down the strip. In passing we saw a few bikes we considered jacking and taking back with us. The only reason we sided against it was because we had already gotten rid of the Harley truck we had drove down in. For most of the day, Treacherous and I just enjoyed being among fellow riders and appreciating the many different bikes we had come across. As night began to fall, I shot back to our motel just ten miles away from the beach and waited for Pete's signal.

* * *

"Yo, dawg, did you see shawdy in the light green with the fatty on the back of dat CBR?" the one Pete described as Mark D asked the kid named Corey passing him the half gallon of Remy.

"You talkin about ole girl with the burgundy hair?" Corey replied.

"Yeah, her."

"Yeah, dat broad was fat."

"Shit, I like the one Black got in da room," Roton said. *"Dat bitch belong in Black Tail magazine."*

"Wait 'til you see the thangs I got comin' through for us later," Kev said.

"I hope they don't look like them monkeys you had up in here two

hours ago," Corey warned.

"Man whatchu talkin' about? Them chicks was straight," Kev said.

"Yeah, straight garbage," Mark D chimed.

Treacherous and I could hear every word as each one of them broke into laughter. Unbeknownst to us Pete had a suite reserved at The Anderson for us to better help execute the plan. He had called Treacherous a couple of hours ago and told us to meet him there. We had arrived just in time to see the female monkeys the crew were all laughing about and their man Black disappearing into the back room. From where we stood we were able to go unnoticed by anyone who might have passed by. We had been waiting for all five men to be visual before we made our move. Treacherous was supposed to text Pete once we had a lock on all five, then he would make his call. Another half an hour went by before the kid named Black reappeared. Treacherous pulled out his phone and texted Pete.

"Damn nigga, you was back there makin' love or something?" Corey was the first to say.

"Never," Black barked with a smile, revealing a mouth full of gold teeth.

"You probably was back there doin' a lot of kissin'," Kev joked.

I could tell by the thick chocolate girl's face she was somewhat embarrassed by the conversation they were having about her right in front of her.

She silently made her way to the door.

"I'mma call you, shawdy," Black shouted just before she shut the door.

"Yeah, call her a bitch or a hoe," Roton quoted from an old Ice Cube song.

"Fuck what you talkin' about, Ro. Dat was some super good pussy right there," Black spit.

"I bet you hit it raw, too, didn't you?" Mark D said.

"Are you serious? You gots to be shittin' me. Cut it out," Black replied.

"Yeah, he did," Corey said, convinced.

Everybody looked at Black at the same time.

A smile appeared across his face. "What? I couldn't help it. The condom was too small."

Once again, all of them joined one another in laughter.

There laughter was interrupted by the sounds of Corey's ring tone.

"Yeah, we in here. Okay, we'll be ready. Suite 1218."

Based on his conversation, Treacherous and I knew it had been Pete on the other end of the line, but Corey's words confirmed it.

"Dat was the nigga Pete. He's on his way over. Bring the money out."

"If we gonna rob him and kill the nigga anyway why we gotta have our money out?" Roton asked.

"Nobody answer him please," Kev requested.

And no one did.

"Mark D, make sure when you pop dat nigga you hit 'em close so the shit won't splatter all over the place and he out for the count," Kev said.

"I got dis."

"Black, you and Corey gonna rap him up in dat plastic we got and get rid of 'em. Ro, you and me gonna secure the money and the dope."

Kev was just about to say something else when they heard the knock at the door. We heard it too.

"What it is, my nigga?" Black greeted Pete at the door.

"Black what's good?" Pete returned.

Everybody said their what's up and gave their handshakes once Pete was in the room. He had a knapsack on his back, which everyone assumed was the drugs.

"Damn. What, y'all was growin' that shit up in here?" Pete complained about the strong odor of marijuana that filled the room. Everybody laughed. They all knew how Pete felt about weed.

"You shot out, cuz," Mark D chimed.

"Yo, that shit killin' me," Pete said, walking over to the sliding door. He stuck his head out and inhaled a breath of salty air coming from the beach.

"You niggas been partying, huh?" Pete said, observing the half of a half gallon of Remy, an empty fifth of Grey Goose, countless bottles of Coors Lights and Coronas, and an almost full bottle of Patron.

"This what we do, dawg," Mark D bellowed.

"Well, this is what I do," Pete shot back, taking off the knapsack. He unzipped the bag. "Y'all check this while I check that." He pointed to the bag containing the money. That was me and Treacherous' cue.

"Yeah, this is what I'm talkin' about," Pete announced as he bent over on the coffee table checking the stacks of money. He never saw Mark D raise his pistol to the back of his head.

Blood sprayed Corey's face from the impact of the shot, but it wasn't whose blood he would have expected. Treacherous slid through the terrace door that Pete had left opened for us, and I followed just in time to catch the kid Mark D drawing his gun. Wasting no time, Treacherous released a clean shot to the back of Mark D's head from his silencer-equipped Beretta. Before anyone could react, Pete had already drawn his hammer and shoved it into Corey.

"No happy ending, muthafucka," he spat as he blew a hole in Corey's chest. The two shots I let loose in rapid succession caught Black in the heart and Roton in the neck. Treacherous swung his gun around in their direction and pumped one more apiece into them. Pete walked up on Kev who was now in shock from the sudden and unexpected bloodshed.

"Is this everything?" Pete asked him.

"Yeah, dawg, dat's everything we had," he answered.

"Good," Pete said then used his piece to brighten up the walls with Kev's brain matter.

Treacherous walked over to where each body lay and lodged another shot into them.

"Let's get the hell up outta here," Pete suggested, snatching up the bag with the drugs and money once Treacherous had reached the final body.

"Nah, you stayin'" Treacherous said to Pete right before he pumped three rounds into his face.

Even I did not expect that but was not surprised. I knew my man had good reason.

Without me having to ask he said, "I didn't like the way the nigga tried to challenge me in front of you at the rest stop."

I had a feeling that was the case because Pete's words didn't sit right with me either when he told Treacherous he would remember that he gave him an invitation for a rematch.

Like always, Treacherous and I made it out in one piece and back to our bikes. We gathered up our belongings, wiped down the motel room and cut our Memorial week short.

CHAPTER EIGHT

Rich stood waiting patiently for his turn to review the next day's pass list. It had been four days since he and O.G. had spoken, and still he had yet to receive the mail O.G. had told him he had sent. It had been weighing heavy on his mind since the second day had gone by. Unable to sleep that night, the next day after he hadn't gotten O.G.'s mail, Rich attempted to call and inform O.G. that nothing had arrived. Up until the time the phones had shut off for the evening Rich made four failed attempts to reach his friend. He would have tried more times than that, but on that particular day the phone lines were extremely hectic due to it being the week of Father's Day. It was not unusual for Rich not to reach O.G. since he had told him the medication the doctor had him on caused him to sleep more often than he'd prefer, so Rich credited him not answering of the phone to just that. As he scanned the pass list for his name, Rich made a mental note to give O.G. a call when he got off from work later. After coming to the fifth page and scrolling down with his finger Rich saw his name was on the list to see his case manager Mr. Brown that morning. He knew the clock was winding down and his release date was nearing so he assumed the scheduled appointment had something to do with his final evaluation and progress reports. Seeing his name on the list put a smile on Rich's face. It had been nearly three decades since he had been in the real world, and now here it was he had survived long enough to return to it. Rich passed the list to the next inmate and made his way back to his area to prepare for his meeting with his case manager.

"Mr. Robinson, you may come in," Mr. Brown said. Rich entered the case manager's office.

"Have a seat." Mr. Brown extended his hand in the direction of the chair that sat in front of his desk. Mr. Brown was a tall, bald by choice, clean shaved, slender but built brown skinned man. He was ex-military, and it showed in his posture. He had army memorabilia spread throughout his office from pictures to plaques. He also had framed awards and degrees he had received throughout the years. The picture of him, his wife and two children displayed on his desk showed he was a family man. Out of all of the other case and unit managers in the institution Mr. Brown was the only one Rich had never heard any other inmates complain or talk about negatively. He had a reputation within the facility of being a fair individual, and Rich was pleased to have been assigned to him.

"How's everything this morning, Mr. Robinson?"

"No complaints," Rich answered.

Mr. Brown smiled. "Robinson, you know that's been your answer to that question since you've been on my caseload."

"That's how it's been for me since I've been on your caseload," Rich replied.

"I always liked you, Robinson."

"I appreciate that."

"I see your time is soon to be coming to an end," Mr. Brown stated, reviewing Rich's prison folder.

"Correct."

"It says in a few months you'll be eligible for the six-month drug program so once you complete that you'll be eligible for the one year time off your sentence and six-month halfway house." Mr. Brown had only confirmed what Rich had already known.

He had long ago calculated the estimated time he would do if he had gotten accepted into the drug program.

"Mr. Robinson, you've been out of society for nearly two and a half decades. That's a long time," Mr. Brown sympathized. "In all the years I've known you I've never asked, but I'm curious to know what your intentions are when you get back out into society."

That was an easy question for him to answer, Rich thought. He only had one intention.

"Just to stay out there and never come back under no circumstances."

"Yeah, I would hope so, but what does that consist of?"

"I just want to live my life," was all Rich offered.

"We received a call the other day from a Mr. Muhammad Bashir, Esquire," Mr. Brown informed him.

The name meant nothing to Rich. He had never heard it mentioned before anywhere.

He sat there in silence with a puzzled expression, waiting for Mr. Brown to continue.

"Mr. Bashir was inquiring as to whether you had received any papers from his firm—important papers that needed to be addressed expeditiously as he put it."

"Are you sure he has the right man, Mr. Brown?" Rich asked.

"Yes he does. We in fact received the papers yesterday. They were sent to you by a Mr. Orlando Goines."

Hearing O.G.'s government name caused Rich to lean forward.

"What papers are you talking about, Mr. Brown?"

"Legal papers."

"If they were legal papers then why was my mail intercepted?" Rich wanted to know. He was fully aware of the institutional policy about mail being subjected to random review or under investigation for suspicious activities. He also knew that normally that applied to gang members or affiliates or anyone who may be accused of selling contraband in the facility such as drugs. Rich knew he didn't fall into any of those categories.

"The mail was put on hold, Mr. Robinson, because the contents didn't go through the proper legal mail procedures such as having you sign for it. Due to Mr. Bashir explaining the importance of the contents, your package was retrieved by the mail sergeant. Rich had noticed the manila envelope on the desk when he first walked in but thought nothing of it. Now that he had been made aware he could see O.G.'s handwriting on the package.

During the time Mr. Brown was updating him as to why his mail sat in front of him, he couldn't help but notice him say, "The importance of the content," twice. His words weren't sitting right with Rich.

"So what did my friend send me that you guys felt I couldn't receive through regular mail?" Rich calmly asked, but on the inside he was becoming irritable.

Mr. Brown smiled and cleared his throat. For a brief moment, he let silence fill the air before he spoke. He was trying to find the right words.

"The contents consisted of a copy of a letter for Power of Attorney and a copy of the last will and testament."

His words wasted no time in registering in Rich's mind.

"When?"

"Four days ago," Mr. Brown answered.

Mr. Brown could not have known his words had just felt like a sledge hammer smashing Rich's heart. It was just four days ago since the last he had spoken to O.G., and now he was gone.

Rich let out a chuckle. "You son of a bitch," he said under his breath. There was no doubt in Rich's mind that his friend knew he would be breathing his last breath after their last conversation on the phone. He shook it off. He knew his friend was now in gangster's paradise and had to suffer no more. Rich knew he'd miss his only friend, but he told himself he'd see him when he too exchanged life on earth for a better place.

"I need you to open the package in front of me," Mr. Brown informed Rich, snapping him back to reality as he handed him the big envelope.

Rich opened it. Inside were the contents Mr. Brown had stated. Rich unfolded them and shook them out for Mr. Brown then handed them to him one at a time. In addition there was a ten-page letter from O.G. Taking a quick glance at the letter the first line only confirmed what Rich had believed to be true.

By the time you receive this scribe I will have already purchased my ticket to the biggest gangster party in history and entered the building.

Those words alone put a huge smile on Rich's face. He folded the letter back up.

"I can take this right?" he asked.

"Of course. This is yours to keep also." Mr. Brown handed the will back to him.

"I just need you to sign these papers so we can have them faxed to Mr. Bashir."

Rich put the will with O.G.'s letter.

"I need something to sign with."

Mr. Brown handed Rich a pen. "Aren't you going to read it first?"

Rich looked at him then took a quick look at the first page of the paper.

"In any event, if something were to happen to me, I leave sole control and power of attorney to my only friend Mr. Richard Robinson."

"I don't need to read it," Rich told Mr. Brown.

"Okay. Mr. Bashir left me with his fax number, so let me get these over to him and give you these back and then you can be on your way."

"No problem."

"And by the way," Mr. Brown said, pausing, "my condolences."

Rich nodded. "Have a good one."

Later that night, when the day had wound down for everyone, Rich lay in his bed and slowly read his friend's final words. He found out O.G. had left him his house, a nice amount of change, and a safety deposit key containing what he felt to be his valuables. After he was finished, Rich pulled out his notepad to write Teflon and tell her he had just lost his only friend.

CHAPTER NINE

It took everything in her power for Teflon not to shed a tear for Rich after reading his letter, but she felt his pain. Outside of herself, Treacherous and his mother, the only other person he had ever spoken about whom he loved and respected was the man he had only referred to in his letters as his friend O.G. Teflon out of all people knew what it was like to lose the one person you loved. She was still dealing with her thoughts and coping with her feelings over the loss of Treacherous after all these years. She knew there was no specific or set amount of time to grieve over a loved one, and she was fine with that. Besides, she had no intentions of ever trying to bury her feelings for her first and only true love. She had told herself when she made a decision to live for a while longer until the two of them met up again she would carry a torch for her only true love.

Rich's letter sent Teflon's mind back to a place where she hadn't revisited since she was a juvenile, causing her to reminisce on the first time she and Treacherous had met. She went into her locker and retrieved a brand-new notepad, sat on her bed, cracked it open, and began to write.

She titled it, "The First Time."

Norfolk Detention Center was jammed with young adolescents and juvenile delinquents. I remember Treacherous telling me how it had taken him no time to find position and gain status in the juvenile jail for young boys and girls. He had been charged with illegal possession of firearms and receiving stolen property. Like me, the judge had called Treacherous a menace to society and a threat to the community and remanded him in the detention center, only he stipulated Treacherous remain in the youth facility until he reached the age of eighteen. To all the other kids who only had to serve a couple weeks, months, or a year or two, what Treacherous had was a juvenile life sentence, so they all respected him for his time. In addition to that, all the wannabe young hustlers and gangsters had discovered that the man they had read about in the newspapers and some knew of and respected was Treacherous' father Richie Gunz.

What they thought about Treacherous made him no difference. His only concern was serving the five-and-a-half years in confinement and how he would pay society back for stripping him of his father as well as his freedom. Some kids learned their lessons and went home better than they came in. Treacherous had never committed a crime in his life prior to the charges he had received and had felt he was being condemned and punished for who his father was and what his father had done, and he was angry at the judicial system. So instead of learning any lessons and going home to become a productive part of society, he made a vow to himself that he would leave up out of there worse than when he entered.

By the time he and I had met, four years had gone by and Treacherous grew both physically and mentally. If he wasn't doing push-ups or dips, he was reading a book. He had gotten his GED two years prior and began to teach himself by acquiring more knowledge through the books that were available to him, which were mostly white historical ones. Treacherous wasn't fortunate to have someone on the outside sending him any good books, but there was one kid who had gotten in a bunch of them by some black authors and he offered Treacherous the opportunity to read them. Treacherous enjoyed reading, especially while he was on room lockdown from fighting. He had told me that prior to us meeting he had a total of twenty-nine fights in the four years he had been in the detention center and won every last one of them. *Whenever Treacherous would get locked down, the kid would slide a book under the door for him. He had read all of the books by Donald Goines and Ice Berg Slim over and over until he practically knew them by heart. He had his favorites like the Kenyatta series and Black Girl Lost, but his all-time favorite was Black Gangsta, all written by Donald Goines. Pimp was his favorite of Ice Berg Slim along with Long White Con.*

It was through these books he had become more educated with the many aspects of the game. He realized, through the books he read, whether you were a pimp, player, con, drug dealer, or a gangsta, you were still a hustler, and you only had two choices, either you go out there and go hard by making it, or you go hard by taking it. From that day forward Treacherous knew what he was going to do upon his release. He told himself the life was in his blood. Treacherous had grown accustomed to the type of attention he received while at The Norfolk Detention Center. It had been his home for the past few years, and he practically ran it. He knew some people spoke out of respect while others spoke out of fear. But either way, I later found out Treacherous gave none of them, male or female, staff or resident, the time of day— no one but me.

He was a loner by nature, and that's the way he liked it. Treacherous had just gotten off room restrictions after being locked down for twenty-one days when he entered the day room. He was eighteen months short of getting his release and decided he would chill this time since his time was quickly coming to an end. As he got his breakfast and sat down, he noticed the young females who had been released from the girls' side to eat.

Initially we were both feeling each other, but what started out as a natural chemistry quickly turned into a war zone. Eventually when war turned into peace he told me over the years girls had come and gone but none had ever really caught his eye prior to me, and I believed him. He said when he first saw me I stood out from the rest, that I looked out of place, and he could see the toughness in my eyes. Treacherous thought I favored his mother slightly. I took that as both an honor and compliment after he had told me the story of his parents.

He said it was the first time he had ever thought someone was worthy of even being compared to his mother. I peeped him staring at me, causing our eyes to meet for a brief moment.

I had only been in the detention center for ten days, but throughout that short period I had practically seen all the guys that had been in there, most of them trying to talk to me, but I wasn't beat. After the first few days of being unsuccessful, they began to view me as stuckup and conceited, which was fine with me. I had heard stories about a kid named Treacherous who had been in detention for four years and stayed on lock down for fighting. I mean everybody was practically on his dick. I was told that he ran the detention center. Now laying eyes on him had me confident he was the one who the girls spoke about, even before the other girls who knew of him had confirmed it.

While everyone else sat at the tables grouped up, Treacherous sat alone and had been doing so for years. Apparently, no one had told me that. Not that it would've made a difference because I had already made up my mind. I headed toward the table where Treacherous was sitting. I could tell he had seen me heading his way because he stopped eating his cereal mid-chew. When I reached his table he looked up at me with piercing eyes. They seemed cold yet wise.

"Is this seat taken?" I asked with what I felt was the deepest but softest voice he had ever heard from a female.

Instead of answering, Treacherous nodded his head. I took that as my cue and sat down. I could see everyone in the dayroom looking at me as I sat with Treacherous. All the boys that were in the detention center were jealous while the girls were envious. Even the staff was in disbelief. No one had bothered to inform me that Treacherous liked to eat alone and expected him to blow up on me, but to their surprise he didn't. I began to feel a little nervous, not because of him but because all eyes were on me—or rather us—and I hated being in the spotlight.

Treacherous continued eating his cereal as I fumbled, trying to open my milk. I hoped that my nervousness in Treacherous' presence didn't show on the outside because on the inside I was a nervous wreck. I had never met a guy who reeked of strength and commanded respect.

I saw how he had the entire facility walking on eggshells. My then ex-boyfriend, who was a bitch-ass nigga and the reason why I was in the detention center in the first place, had been the leader of his block, but he was not respected or feared the way I had felt he should have been. I was only fifteen at the time, but my ex was nineteen. As sharp as I thought I was, I couldn't believe how naïve I had been when it came to him, and now I was sitting up in jail for him.

I continued to fight with the milk carton as Treacherous watched me out the corner of his eye. Later he revealed, he was tempted to help me but he just couldn't bring himself to do it. That was not his style. He was a gangsta, and gangstas kept it gangsta at all times. Just then I was able to get my fingernail in the lip, thinking I had the difficult milk carton licked, but as I peeled the flaps open, the dumbest shit happened. The milk slipped out of my hands.

"Oh shit, my bad," I quickly chimed, seeing the milk had spilled over the table toward Treacherous. He jumped up just as the milk began pouring in his lap. Everyone saw the commotion and turned their attention toward me and Treacherous.

"Clumsy ass chick," Treacherous shouted as he brushed the milk off the front of his jumper.

I was just about to apologize for my mistake until I was interrupted by the words that came out of his mouth.

"What? Fuck you," I retorted. "It was a mistake. Who the fuck you calling clumsy?"

All the other girls and guys were now looking at me as if I had lost my mind. The other kids were sure now Treacherous was going to knock my teeth down my throat for the blatant disrespect. They had never heard anyone take that tone with Treacherous.

Treacherous looked at me as if my words lashed at him. Before he could even do or say anything, staff ran and jumped between the two of us.

"Mr. Freeman, please go over there," one of the staff members requested, pleading with him while the other staff tried to escort me out of the dining area.

Treacherous knew why they were handling him in such a manner.

On several occasions throughout his stay at the detention center, Treacherous had become untamable whenever altercations arose with him and another resident. The situation with me was actually Treacherous' first time ever getting into a situation with a female. What the staff could not have known was no matter what I had said to him, Treacherous would never put his hands on me.

Treacherous did as he was told and backed up as he watched me carry on.

"Get your fucking hands off me, bitch," I screamed as I punched one of the female staffers in the midsection. Another one tried to calm me down, only to be met with my fist to her jaw, sending her to the floor. That's when two male staff grabbed me from behind. Even they had a hard time with me. Later, when he came home, Treacherous would sometimes tease me on how feisty and rowdy of a girl I was when I was younger.

"Why y'all catering to that muthafucka I didn't do shit," I yelled as I kicked and scratched all the way out the dayroom.

Everyone laughed at the performance—everyone except Treacherous. He had never met a female like me and admired my tenacity. He said he loved the way I fought for what I believed in and was able to say what others wished they could have said to him regardless of any consequences or repercussions. He told me about a quote he had read in a book that had stuck with him: "If you don't stand for something then you'll fall for anything." He knew I was only standing up for what I believed in. After everything had died down, Treacherous went back to his room where he felt most comfortable, picked up a book, and read it. He said that night he stayed in his room and thought about me. Back then he referred to me as the crazy girl who had resembled his mother who just caused so much trouble. Based on the stories his father had told him about her, he said he could see I also shared his mother's fire.

While eating lunch, he came across my name from the discussion the other girls were having at the table across from him. Treacherous thought the name Teflon to be peculiar for a girl, he told me, but then again wondered who was he to talk about names? His father had given him the reason behind his name, and he wondered what had possessed my parents to give me such a name. I lie across the bed with my arms folded, locked inside the little six-by-nine room and thought about how I had gotten there, but I knew the answer to that: from dealing with a little boy who thought he was the man. That and being in the wrong place at the wrong time. The ending result was me being sentenced to sixteen months in Norfolk Detention House for possession with intent and aggravated assault with a weapon.

I didn't mind being charged with the assault because I was guilty of that.

I and my then boyfriend were just coming home after having an enjoyable dinner and evening at a popular restaurant in downtown Norfolk. As I unlocked my home and opened the door, I didn't think anything of the darkness as we entered the two-bedroom condo my boyfriend had purchased for me as a birthday present in my name under the table. As I reached for the light to illuminate my domain, me and my boyfriend were met with badges, guns, and a barrage a yelling. Both me and my boyfriend did as we were told and hit the ground quick and fast. When the officer approached us with the packaged drugs and asked the unforgettable question of whose drugs it was, looking over to my boyfriend, confident he would step up to the plate, something he had always preached, I could not believe her ears.

"That shit ain't mine. I don't live here. I'm just visiting my girl." You would have thought he was Denzel Washington the way words came out of his mouth. My now ex-boyfriend would always remember how he had did me dirty every time he looked in the mirror and saw the scar on his face that ran from the side of his eye down to the corner of his mouth, compliments of my blade which I use to keep in my mouth at all times, the way I used to see my mother do. Far from being a dummy, seeing that the fix was in, I spit the razor into my hand just as quick as any veteran on Rikers Island and caught my ex across the face good enough to send him to the hospital for one hundred fifty stitches known as a buck fifty. The police Maced me with pepper spray to subdue me *and carried me off to detention while they took my ex to the hospital.*

He was charged with the drugs in the house as well but posted bail, and because I refused to tell who the drugs really belonged to and my ex had already given his statement, he beat his case and I wore the weight. I couldn't bring myself to snitch on somebody. It just wasn't in my blood. I was and still am a ride or die bitch, so I took the sixteen months they gave me and maintained my integrity and self-respect, compromising neither of the two. Neither of my parents were ever really there for me or told me anything to prepare me for the life that lay ahead of me, but what I knew about them both, I assumed they played the game fair, each playing their role and position.

As I lay in the bed that night I couldn't help but think about Treacherous. It wasn't my intention to beef with him the way I had, but he had caught my vein. I had an issue with the way people talked to me, males in particular, and still do. My mother had instilled that inside of me, and there was no exception to the rule. Besides, all that was built up inside of me from my ex was released and directed toward him. It took me a day to take it down and cool off to realize I wasn't even mad at him. I had no right to be because I barely knew him other than what I had heard about him. He must think I'm crazy, I thought as I dwelled on the situation. I couldn't figure back then why was I so concerned about what he thought about me. I had no clue, but I had promised myself when my forty-five-day room restriction was up I would step to him again, only with a different approach. I lay back in the six-by-nine room's bed and closed my eyes that night. Images of my childhood haunted me, invading my mind as I slipped into a trance and began to relive my past.

After my forty-five days of room restriction had ended I was all too ready to see Treacherous again and start all over. Being in the room for so long and just eating and resting had put a few pounds on me, filling out my 112-pound frame into an even 120 pounds, all eight pounds going into the right places. My hair had also grown at least two-and-a-half inches from keeping it in two braids, but that day I wore it all pulled back in one big ponytail, which showed off long wavy hair. I had actually enjoyed my little room vacation. It gave me time to gather my thoughts, and now that I had gotten them together I wanted to be allowed to interact with the others, one person in particular.

Treacherous later admitted he had scratched my last day of room lock date off his calendar as soon as he woke. He had been counting down the forty-five days they had given me. Throughout that time he had done less reading and more working out, trying to get better toned. He had always had a nice chiseled physique, but he told me I became his motivation. It was something about me that caused him to want to work out harder. He went from doing a thousand push-ups a day to doing fifteen hundred, along with increasing his crunches from 750 a day to a thousand, adding to his washboard stomach. When he had weighed himself two days before, he had gone up from 170 pounds to 182 pounds solid with only 10 percent body fat. During my room lock he had packed on twelve pounds of bulk.

The staff was a little leery about allowing me to return to general population, especially not knowing how Treacherous would react to seeing me again, so they decided to monitor our behavior closely and prepare for anything. The last thing they wanted to see was Treacherous half killing me, but I wasn't worried about anything like that. My only concern was that he wouldn't want to hear me out.

All the other inmates had been doing their own counting down of my release, placing bets on how long it would take for me to go back into lockup or get strangled by Treacherous, betting their breakfast, lunch, and dinner trays. The detention center had gotten live in the past month and a half. Some kids from Norfolk had gotten arrested in a drug raid and smuggled some weed inside, and six new girls, three who were young prostitutes, had came up in there, so everybody was trying to get in on the action.

Some were even taking chances sliding up in the bathroom or one of the classrooms with them unnoticed, sexing the young prostitutes. But Treacherous wasn't concerned with any of that. He didn't get high nor did he trick. He did take the weed though and stashed it in a book he knew nobody would touch because none of the kids up in there really read books.

All the girls were attracted to Treacherous and tried to entice him in hopes of becoming his jailhouse girlfriend by flashing their breasts at him and propositioning him, but he was only interested in one girl. Treacherous sat at his regular table by himself as he saw the young girls lined up coming from off the female side. In total, including me, there were now eleven girls, which was the most Treacherous had ever seen in the juvenile facility at one time the whole four years and some change he had been there.

For a minute, Treacherous thought I had not been a part of the female lineup and wondered where I was, but right before the door had fully closed, he saw me.

I came through the door with that same style and grace I thought sparked the look Treacherous had on his face when he first laid eyes on me, still looking as if I didn't belong in such a place. As I entered the dining area, our eyes met just like before. Treacherous tried to play it off and act as if it was just coincidence that he happened to look my direction, but I knew better. He couldn't help but to notice how good those forty-five days were to me. Having two good eyes he couldn't help but notice how I had blossomed into something even more beautiful while in isolation, seeing that I had put on a few pounds in all the right places and how my hair had even grown. One of the girls had noticed the inconspicuous way Treacherous was looking at me.

"Girl, that nigga checkin' you out," the girl volunteered.

"Mind your fucking business," I swung around and snapped, irritated by the girl's nosiness.

The girl started to snap back with a sly remark but thought better of it. I continued to watch Treacherous as he glided to his usual spot. My heart skipped a beat. Treacherous sat there at the very same table he had been sitting at the first time I had ever seen him, only this time he was much bigger. He could have easily passed for a Greek god or a poster child for a muscle magazine, I thought, seeing the indentions of his physique through his shirt as his trap muscles sat up just below his ears.

Although we didn't realize it at that time—or rather we didn't give a fuck—all eyes were on us. Everyone wanted to see the outcome of Treacherous and Teflon's reunion. Some kids snickered under their breaths, anticipating the worse, while others who bet in favor of Treacherous humbling himself thought the opposite. Staff was just ready for whatever either way it went. It was their job to secure the safety of the institution and that was their only concern.

I got breakfast and began looking around as if I was in search of a seat, but it was only to buy me some time to get my thoughts together and decide whether I really wanted to go through with my intentions, because I already knew where I intended to eat. One of the guys who tried to push up on me when I first arrived motioned for me to sit with him and his clown ass friends, but I acted as if I hadn't seen him. I made up my mind and walked toward my intended destination.

I noticed Treacherous observing me as I pretended to look around for a place to sit. He started to motion for me to come and chill with him, but thought better of it, because he knew that wasn't gangsta, but I could see in his facial expression that he wasn't feelin' it when he saw the punk kid to his right try to get me to come chill with him and his punk-ass boys. He told me his blood began to boil and he wanted to take his food tray and bash the kid in the face. Honestly, I would've loved to see him do it. It would've turned me on and just made me want him more. At the sight of me ignoring them and heading toward him, he began to calm down, but had I accepted the punk kid's invitation, he said he would've gotten up, went over there, and followed through with his first thought just on general principle. As childish as it may have seemed, that's just how Treacherous got down.

Everybody watched as I stopped in front of Treacherous' table.

"Can I sit here?" I asked with confidence.

"Go ahead. It ain't mine," Treacherous replied nonchalantly.

Hearing Treacherous' voice did something to me. The baritone sound made me want to surrender to him in every way possible but I maintained my composure as I sat down.

Treacherous was not use to talking to females, so he didn't really know what to say to me, he later confessed. The only thing he could strike up a conversation about was jail things, but he didn't want to discuss that because he was living it, so why talk about it? He wondered if he should start with an apology, but quickly erased the thought because he didn't owe me one. The thought of everyone staring at him caused him to clinch his teeth. He didn't have to look around to know that they were. He could feel their eyes all on the side of his face. He continued to eat his breakfast thinking of where to begin.

I thought about what I would say to Treacherous the whole forty-five days I was on room restriction. I had rehearsed my opening over and over until it sounded right to me, but as I sat before him, all I had rehearsed faded out of my mind, and my thoughts became a blur. I noticed all the other girls were staring at me like I was crazy. Rather than black out on them and risk going back to lockup before I accomplished what I set out to do, I gave them a pass and rolled my eyes at them. You would've thought Treacherous and I were playing the leading role in a drama movie the way everyone was focused on us. I knew even if Treacherous wanted to say something to me first, he wouldn't because his reputation was on the line, so I knew I would have to be the one to initiate it. I took a deep breath then exhaled.

"Um, Treach."

Hearing my soft-toned voice speak his name caused Treacherous to stop eating and look up. He had no idea I had possessed such a beautiful and smooth voice. On the last encounter I had sounded just as rough, if not rougher than the average dude in there when I stood up to him, he thought.

I knew I now had his attention hearing me say his name, so I continued.

"I want to apologize for what I'm—"

"You don't owe me any apology," Treacherous interrupted me.

"That shit wasn't about—"

I cut him back off. "Yes it was about something. I had no right flippin' out on you like that that day. I ain't even—"

"Hold on, shortie," Treacherous interrupted again. "Yo mind your muthafuckin' business," he barked to all who had been paying close

attention to us, some even leaning out of their seats. Everyone began to act as if they were involved in something other than our conversation.

I smiled on the inside at how Treacherous had checked the whole dayroom. Even the staff began to mind their business after hearing the power and strength behind Treacherous' words. It was apparent that rather than a problem, there was a connection between the two of us.

"My bad, pardon me. What were you sayin'?"

I continued. "I was just sayin' I ain't even know you like that to be screamin' on you the way I did, and it was my bad. I know you got a lot of time up in here and a lot of respect, more than I ever seen one man have, and I wanted you to know I didn't mean to disrespect you because like everybody else, I respect you too."

Treacherous looked me in my eyes as I spoke, and I never broke his stare. Even most of the dudes he had come across who professed to be thorough could not hold a stare as long as I had when I spoke. Treacherous knew I was not like any other female he had ever known. Most girls always showed a sign of weakness or vulnerability, but even in my apology Treacherous detected nothing but strength and security. He was intrigued to know more about me.

"Yo, I respect you for respecting me enough to get at me like this, but that shit we went through is over just like the forty-five days you just did. I could've handled the situation differently, too, but it is what it is, you know what I'm sayin'? We cool, ain't no beef, and if you have any problems while you up in here let me know. I don't care if it's inmates or staff, I got your back," Treacherous stated firmly.

"And I got your back too," I replied.

Treacherous looked at me awkwardly, then shot me a half smile that only I caught.

"A'ight, I respect that."

I shot him the same half grin.

"A'ight, shortie, I'll catch you later. You cutting' into my reading time," Treacherous said, getting up from the table.

I did not want him to leave, but I understood he had a set schedule.

Before I left up out of there I intended to become a part of his daily schedule as well. It had dawned on me that we hadn't been properly introduced.

"Wait," I called out as Treacherous began walking away.

"What up?"

"You don't even know my name."

"Yes, I do, Miss Teflon Jackson," Treacherous replied before walking away, but that was the last time he would ever walk away from me because from that day forward Treacherous and I were inseparable.

Six months later things between Treacherous and I had strengthened beyond anyone's imagination, and no one but us liked it. Other male inmates hated and despised Treacherous from afar because they wanted to be him while they lusted over me. The female inmates who once thought they had a chance with Treacherous felt the same way but they knew better. It was no secret that I would hurt something over him. Every so often, a new girl was gassed up or one of the regulars built up enough heart and nerve to step to Treacherous, only to feel the wrath of me, who didn't play when it came to Treacherous. Before my sentence at the detention center was complete, I had received room restriction on three separate occasions, badly injuring three girls who tried to move in on my man.

Staff thought me to be a bad influence on Treacherous. Often they tried to separate the two of us to no avail. They even went as far as trying to get Treacherous transferred to the county jail but never had good reason to because he never gave them one. Ever since I had come into the picture Treacherous had been reserved and humble. He tried to keep me at bay but couldn't control my temper when it came to my jealousy. Treacherous assured me he only had eyes for me. To prove it, he carved a set of eyes in his arm with my name overtop with the metal part of a number two pencil.

Although I believed Treacherous' every word, I didn't trust other women. My motto was what was mine was mine, and Treacherous belonged to me. Treacherous went through hell every time I was locked down. He enjoyed my company and conversation and missed it when-

ever I got into trouble. We would talk about what we were going to do together when we were both released. The days couldn't go by quick enough for Treacherous, but they were steadily approaching, he knew. I would be released first but Treacherous knew he wouldn't be too far behind.

I was on room lock once again, and though he missed me, Treacherous was heated with me. He tried to defuse the situation that caused me to be confined to my room, but I wouldn't listen, and now after my room lock was over, in sixty days I would be going home, and Treacherous knew he wouldn't see me again until his release. Treacherous later told me how disappointed he was at me and had played the tape back that lead to my predicament. I remembered it as if it were yesterday. This incident was inevitable because some bitches are just hardheaded and are going to try you anyway until you show them, your not to be fucked with. Her name was Carmen and she was from Richmond.

Carmen was the newest female in the detention center. She was an attractive Hispanic sixteen-year-old who was caught shoplifting in Military Circle Mall.

"Hey, Treach," she chimed, approaching Treacherous as he played solitaire.

"What do you want, Carmen?" Treacherous asked, not bothering to look up. He knew Carmen liked him, but he paid her no mind. She stood five feet nine inches tall with still room to grow. Her hair was black with blond highlights, which matched her smooth skin tone. Both her body and facial features favored the Latina singer Shakirah. Treacherous later confessed after I whipped her ass that he would have to turn away from her because she constantly flashed her 34Cs at him whenever I wasn't around. Once, Treacherous noticed Carmen fondling herself while licking her lips, which always seemed as if they were laced with MAC lip gloss. Even if he wasn't with me, Treacherous had told me he was not attracted to Carmen's demeanor.

"You," she boldly answered.

"Get out of here, Carmen, 'fore you get yourself in something you can't get out of," Treacherous warned her. This bitch wouldn't take a hint though.

Carmen knew exactly what Treacherous was insinuating. She figured if she could be viewed as being just as hard as me then maybe Treacherous would choose her over my ass. Little did she know she was wrong.

"I know you don't think somebody scared of that chick. Maybe these other puntas is, but not me, sweetheart. I'm Boriqua. I ain't from around here. I'm from Richmond—the projects, baby!" Carmen announced.

Right at that moment, I was returning from the rest room. Instantly I zeroed in on Carmen hovering over Treacherous. My heart raced with anger. I remembered what Treacherous had said about my temper and tried to calm myself. I wanted to spend my remaining two months left with him before I was released. I could see everyone watching as I made my way over to Carmen and Treacherous.

"Yeah, papi, I bet you never had your dick sucked the way I could suck."

That was all I had to hear to make me spring into action.

Being Hispanic made it convenient for me to grab a fistful of Carmen's long silky hair. Carmen never saw it coming. I flung her around so rapidly and forcefully that she got whiplash.

"Ugh" she said as she hit the floor. I immediately pounced on top of Carmen. I intended to make an example out of her as I commenced to pounding on her beautiful pecan face. I wanted all the other females in the detention center to see what they'd be facing when they got released if I heard they tried to move in on Treacherous while I was gone. By the time the slaughter was over, both of my hands were swollen from the beating I had put on Carmen while both of Carmen's eyes were purple. She had swallowed two teeth and was treated for a fractured collarbone from the fall.

The day I was released, one of the girls I knew was trustworthy delivered a letter from me to Treacherous. It would be the last letter he would receive from me before I was released. Treacherous told me he went to his room and locked himself in. The letter was folded as small as possible, taped on all four corners. I had tried my best to secure it.

Whenever I would receive room lock, Treacherous and I would write each other and send our letters through the same girl. Each time he opened one of my notes it always started out the same: "For your eyes only." That was one of the things he admired and had grown to love about me.

Treacherous finally opened up what would be his last letter from me. He had told me specifically not to write when I got out. I was disappointed at first until he explained how once we were released there was no looking back. Confinement would be a thing of the past. The next time we would see or hear from each other we would both be free of bondage. That night Treacherous told me he lay back on his bunk and opened the yellow lined paper and read my letter.

Hey baby,

I know you're probably still mad at me, but don't be. You know how I am when it comes to you. I told you before, I tried to keep my cool like you always tell me to, but I couldn't let that one slide. That was just total disrespect. That chick had it coming to her anyway. I think I did good 'cause I never said anything, but I knew she used to be flashing you and playing with herself when I wasn't around. Yeah, you didn't think I knew that. Our mail carrier use to tell me. I had her watching you. She told me you used to be turning your head. Lucky for you (smile). But when I heard her talking about putting you in her mouth and all of that, that was it. She had to get it. Besides, I'm the only one who's going to be doing that. Yeah, I said it.

I can't wait until you come up out of that hell hole. I remember everything we talked about, but by the time you get here I will have already gotten a few things established for us. I know you told me don't worry about that other thing, but baby, trust me, I got it. That muthafucka owe and he gonna pay, one way or another. I don't have to tell you to hold your head in there because you were doing that before we met. I think that's what attracted me to you—in fact I know. Those eighteen months being in there with you were the best months of my life, and I wouldn't change them for nothing. I hope you feel the same. You better, nigga (smile). So, this is it, our last letter. Baby, it's

been real, and it's gonna get even realer when you hit the bricks. Until
then...love you!
      'Til Death Do Us Part,
      Your Ride or Die Chick

Treacherous never responded to the letter, but when I met him out-
side when he was released that letter was one of the only things he'd
left the detention center with. From that day forward the reign of Treach-
erous and Teflon began.

Teflon closed the note pad after ending the latest excerpt, pulled out the
one she used to write letters, and began responding to Rich.

CHAPTER TEN

Six years later...

"You have a pre-paid call from Teflon Jackson, from a federal correctional facility. Your call may be recorded or monitored. To accept this call, press five. To refuse this call, hang up. To block this caller from future calls, press pound, pound."

"Hey, baby girl," Rich greeted, accepting Teflon's call.

"Hey," she replied.

As always, Rich could hear the frustration in her tone. It was the same frustration he had detected and had been hearing for nearly six months, since he had been released from prison and had the phone turned on so he and Teflon could communicate. It tore Rich up inside the first time he'd spoken to her over the phone.

In her letters throughout the years of their corresponding, she'd always sound so strong to Rich, but despite her trying to maintain that same sense of strength over the phone, her voice came across as that of a woman whose spirits were breaking by the day and patience was wearing thin. It bothered him, knowing there wasn't anything he could really do to change her current situation, as fast as he would have liked to. Since he had been released, the moment his feet touched the pavement of Virginia's streets, Rich had dedicated his time to the two promises he had made Teflon: One, to locate his grandson, and two, find representation to handle Teflon's appeal. He had made progress on them both, but not enough to satisfy him or make him want to share with Teflon. Luckily for him O.G. had left him enough money to tide him over as well as a place to call home upon his release, or else it would have been that much more difficult to do anything for Teflon or himself for that matter. Rich often wondered what it would have been like for him, at his age coming home to nothing. As the thought crossed his mind, Rich shook it off and re-focused on his phone call

"I see you got the money I sent to put on the phone."

"Yeah, thanks, but the rest I could've done without," Teflon retorted, referring to the additional two hundred dollars Rich had sent on top of the two hundred he sent for the phone.

"What I tell you about talkin' crazy?" he shot back. He knew she was going to say something about the extra money. Since he'd been home, he had sent her money for the phone and prison necessities.

"And don't try to send it back either, like you did before cause I'mma send it right back."

That got a slight chuckle out of Teflon.

"You think you know me, ole man?"

Rich always smiled at the title he had grown accustomed to.

"I think I've known you long enough to say I do, wouldn't you say?"

"You already know the answer to that," Teflon replied.

Rich expected as much. He was use to not getting straight answers from Teflon when it came to questions about how close they'd become throughout the nine-and-a-half years they'd bonded.

"I love you, too, daughter-in-law," he offered.

It was Teflon's turn to smile.

Hearing those words coming from Rich were always comforting to her. Whenever he addressed her as daughter-in-law, it always caused her to think about Treacherous and how legally she would have been Rich's daughter-in-law had his son still been alive. She reflected on the first time she and Rich had spoken on the phone. She couldn't believe her ears. Had she not known better she would have sworn that it was Treacherous. Their voices were almost identical, sharing the same baritone but raspy voice. It took some getting used to for her in the beginning. Talking to Rich was very emotional for Teflon at first. It was as if Treacherous had been reincarnated, but after awhile she began to notice the difference. Where Rich's voice became subtle, at times Treacherous' had always remained hard, even in the midst of expressing himself. Both men spoke with conviction and passion, but Rich's words were those of a much wiser man with an older soul. His life experiences revealed themselves in their conversations. Every so often, Rich would say something that sounded as if he were quoting Treacherous verbatim over the phone.

"So when you gonna ship me that book?" Rich asked, bringing Teflon back to the present "You've been promising to send it to me for a minute now. Don't tell me you're slacking up in there."

"Never that," she replied. "It's just that it's so hard to let go. I must've read it a hundred times since I finished it and…well it's just real personal for me, you know."

"I understand. That's like my only connection to my son too. From your writing, I got to see a side of him I never got to experience, you feel me? Anyway, I started reading some of those street lit books just to compare to your work and you're just as good if not better than some of these authors out here," Rich complimented.

"Why you comparing me to them? I'm not trying to be no author. They ain't no different than rappers. Most of what they write either somebody told them or they was on the porch watching. They don't come from where we do. Seriously, I'm not impressed with that street lit shit," Teflon said.

"This story is for me, your grandson, and for you, nobody else. This is my life—our life. They talk it, we lived it," Teflon chimed.

"Relax, daughter-in-law," an understanding Rich replied. "No one's trying to turn you into an author. I was just letting you know how good I thought your work was. You got skills, that's all."

"Thanks, ole man," a more calm Teflon cooed, embracing Rich's compliment. "And my bad."

"For what?"

"For basing at you."

"Is that what you were doing?" Rich asked, making light of the situation.

"Not intentionally," Teflon answered.

"Sounded kinda soft to me."

"Whateva, ole man. Ain't nuthin' soft about me. You're the one getting soft in your old age," she quickly shot back at Rich. The two of them both shared a laugh, then a sudden silence filled the air.

"I miss him," Teflon said, breaking the silence.

"Me, too, baby girl," Rich said.

"Ha." She chuckled. "He used to call me that sometimes. You sounded just like him. And the funny thing is I never use to like it or that boo stuff, which he always called me, but I never told him that. I knew he meant it out of love, but I just loved the way it sounded when he called me babe or just Tef. His voice was so raspy that when he called my name it sounded like he was calling me tough. Damn I miss his ass…" Her voice faded as her emotions began to well up.

Rich smiled. He could hear the love in Teflon's tone as she spoke about his deceased son. The strength of their bond and love was obvious, even to a blind man. Whenever Teflon spoke of Treacherous, just as he reminded her of his son, she reminded Rich of Teresa. "You sound like his mother sometimes to me," Rich stated, "not your voice, but the love in it whenever you speak about my son. Teresa use to worship the ground I walked on and loved me more than the word itself. At first, I use to think it was because I had been there for her when she needed someone to be there the most, but it was more than that—it ran deeper. I never told you the story of how she and I met. Hell, I never even told my son, but without going into depth over the phone, she had proven to be my rider from day one and 'til the day she breathed her last breath. All the way up until the day my son was born, that's all she had ever been," Rich ended.

It was difficult to relive the past concerning Teresa. His only memories of a woman or love for that matter aside from his time with Treacherous were only of Teresa. Back then, he knew he was not in touch with his inner feelings nor was he an expressive man. It wasn't until he had gone to prison that he'd discovered how painful love could be and how he had deprived himself of the beauty and luxuries of it.

He couldn't help but to think about the time Treacherous had come to visit him for the first and ultimately the last time while he was in prison. It was because he had raised Treacherous to show no emotions that when he himself showed them his son had taken it as a sign of weakness, something that was as foreign to him coming from his father and caused him to cut off all contact with him. As a result, his son shunned him. Thought he was a weakling and wanted nothing more to do with Rich. It pained Rich to know that he had created that emotionless being and it haunted him. It continued to haunt him to this very day.

"Shit, look at us." Rich laughed, pulling himself together.

"I know, right," Teflon agreed. "But we can't help who we love though."

"I know that's right."

"Anyway, I finally found a lawyer to take your case." Rich changed the subject.

Teflon did not respond. Rich knew she had practically given up hope on coming home, but he was determined to try with all his being. He had seen some of the most airtight convictions get reversed, so he knew anything was possible when dealing with the judicial system.

"He said you have some good arguments," he said. "I'll keep you posted."

"Have you found out anything about your grandson yet?" It was Teflon who now switched the subject.

"Still working on it," was all Rich offered.

"You have one minute remaining," the automated voice system interrupted.

"Okay, I'm gonna go, but I enjoyed talking to you as always. Love is love," Teflon said, wrapping up their call.

Like always, whenever he heard her speak the familiar words, he grew silent. "Me too," he replied, clearing his throat. "Okay. 'Til the next time, hold ya head and stay a rider."

"Always. You too."

CHAPTER ELEVEN

"Breaking news just in. Police have arrested two Newport News men in connection to yet another bank robbery in the downtown area of Richmond after gun battle erupted between five men and authorities. Two of the suspects were pronounced dead on the scene while police are in search of the fifth member of the attempted heist getaway who sources are saying may have fled the scene of the crime with an estimated one hundred thousand dollars. At least three of the men, including one of the deceased, had criminal records and the two captured and two deceased all bore gang-affiliated tattoos. Although police have not confirmed, sources are saying this may very well have been another case of an initiation into one of the surrounding gangs that continue to sweep the Virginia area."

"Little dumb asses." Rich shook his head in disgust as he watched the botched robbery. Since he had been home, not a day had gone by on the news that something about banks or gangs flashed across the screen. Ever since he had witnessed his son's demise on television while he was still incarcerated and because gangs didn't exist in his day, the reports left a bad taste in his mouth. Based on what Teflon had shared with him of her and his son's last caper, Rich believed Treacherous had actually sat down and tried to plan a foolproof job despite the final outcome, but did not believe the recent bank robberies he heard about on the news had been thoroughly thought out.

Rich believed he was one of Virginia's most notorious ex-robber. He had caught some of the best of them slipping in the game and had pulled off some of Virginia's most talked about and unsolved capers in history. Rich shook his head, grinning at the thought as he reflected on one of his most infamous heists, which was thought to be impossible, in his robbery career. He knew he'd take to his grave.

***

Leslie Tyler aka Big Les cautiously turned onto the street he routinely turned onto every Thursday night. This time in his cream Mark V with the plush eggshell-white leather interior and matching white wall tires. He owned a fleet of Caddys from Fleetwoods to Devilles, compliments of the numbers and dope houses he had spread throughout the city of Portsmouth. Out of force of habit, he adjusted his rearview mirror as he checked to see he was possibly being followed. This was what he was accustomed to doing ever since his spot on Harrison Street became his number one cash cow house. Being a naturally paranoid man combined with the cocaine he snorted, Big Les was always careful when he was visiting the house.

Each week for the past three months he made it a point to switch up the vehicles he used to pick up deliveries, taking back streets and circling the surrounding area three to four times before actually considering going to his money-making spot.

Convinced the coast was clear, Big Les cruised up the street toward the house. Once he arrived, he pulled into the driveway of a beige-and-brown three-family house. To someone looking from the outside, one would assume the home appeared to be a nice place to live but behind closed doors, they could have never imagined another world existed—a world of negativity.

Big Les shut off the light on the Mark V and continued to drive toward the back part of the house. He then killed the car's engine. Before exiting, he raised the medallion, which hung from his gold Italian link chain and twisted it slightly to the side, exposing the white powdered substance. Big

Les then took his pinky fingernail and scooped the cocaine up. He sniffed half the powder up one nostril then repeated the act with the other. Again, he checked his rearview mirror. Noticing he had white powder residue in the creases of his nostrils, Big Les wiped his nose with his fingers. The cocaine began to take an immediate effect on him. He wiped the residue from his fingers onto his gums, instantly numbing them. He took a piece of spearmint gum out the wrapper he had taken out of his inside blazer and popped it in his mouth. He then reached over to the glove compartment, unlocked it, and snatched up the .38 police special he concealed and shoved it into his belt. He took one final glance to ensure he had everything before he opened the car door and got out. Normally when he visited the other houses, he'd conceal his weapon by buttoning his blazer, but in his main house recently Big Les had been keeping it out in the open as a form of intimidation toward his workers. They were pulling in too much money for him, and instilling fear in them was the only way Big Les felt he could prevent any of them from crossing him or trying to rob him.

The cocaine now in full effect, Big Les felt like King Kong ready to take on Godzilla.

He took one last look over in the reflection of the Mark V's window. He was a neat freak, and the drug had him thinking that something was out of place. He began to brush himself off, starting with his shoulders down to the legs of his pants. When he came back up, he saw what was really out of place in the reflection of the car window. He wanted to react but his reflexes failed him.

"Don't be stupid, hero," Rich warned him, unarming him of the pistol in his waistband.

"This is some kind of joke, right?" Big Les laughed.

"You're the only joke, Les," Rich retorted.

Hearing his name did something to Big Les. Between the cocaine in his system and his big ego he was not in the least bit afraid.

"Nigga, you know who I am, and you still got the nerve to pull this shit. You must be suicidal."

"Whateva you say," Rich said before punching Big Les in the back with a pair of brass knuckles he had on his left hand.

Big Les went crashing to the ground on one knee. He looked up just in time to see the masked gunman delivering a blow with the brass knuckles aimed at his jawline.

Rich heard the sound of teeth cracking as the punch landed on the side of Big Les' face. Rich went to deliver another blow only to be stopped by the wave of Big Les' hand.

"You got it, my man. Whatever you want," he surrendered through a bloodied mouth. Big Les was leaking like a faucet. Rich knew he had broken the big man down.

"This is what I want you to do," Rich said.

Once Rich filled Big Les in on what was expected of him, he escorted him up to the stash house.

"Who?" someone asked, recognizing the secret knock.

"Who you?" was Big Les' response. Under any other circumstances he would have made an attempt to alarm his worker who stood on the other side of the door with a double barreled sawed-off shotgun, but he couldn't take the chance of getting hit in the process or furthermore being killed by the gunman standing on the side of him. The worker began unlocking the four bolts on the stash house's steel door. When he opened it up, he was met with a revolver pointed at his head.

"Easy, big man. Don't be a hero. It's not your money," Rich said in a low tone, unarming him of the shotgun. He noticed how big the man was and knew he'd have to take his life fast if he even blinked too many times.

"Do as he says, Tiny," Big Les instructed.

Tiny saw the damage done to Big Les' face and knew the man with the gun pointed at him meant business. He did as he was told. Rich couldn't help but laugh to himself at the big man's monarch.

"Here, tie him up," Rich told Big Les, handing him the duct tape. "And cover his mouth too."

Once that was done, Rich stuffed the big man into a corner out of plain view.

"Hey, boss," the worker posted up by the door greeted. He didn't even notice the bruises on Big Les' face due to the dimness of the hallway.

"What's happenin', Major?"

He never got to answer nor did he see Rich come up from his blind side.

"I'ma tell you like I told ya boy Tiny, be easy and don't be a hero. It's not your money," Rich repeated, putting the barrel of his gun to the man's temple.

Without realizing it, Major's beige Swedish knit pants became soiled with urine.

"You got it, blood." Major threw up his hands.

Big Les couldn't believe he had such a coward in his camp.

"You know the drill," Rich said to Big Les. He performed the same treatment on Major that he had on Tiny.

Once Rich secured Major he instructed Big Les to open the door. He had already given him the layout and what to expect on the other side, and Rich was prepared. If anything looked any different than what was told to him Rich had already made up his mind that Big Les would be the first to die. When the door opened, all Big Les' workers were surprised to see him. They were even more surprised when they saw Rich appear. Some were off to the right playing a game of spades while exchanging sticks of weed and sipping on beer and liquor while one man and two women, all three in the nude with face masks were off to the left in the kitchen area bottling product. Two men were sitting on an old sofa directly in front counting stacks of money with two guns and a bunch of rubber bands on the table and duffle bags beside them. Before anyone had time to react, Rich sprang into action

"Everybody relax," he suggested, coming up behind Big Les with one revolver pointed at his head and the other scanning the area. Despite it seeming as if everyone in the room was going to comply Rich knew there was going to be one who would rebel. Just as he figured, as soon as the rebel emerged from the table in front of him and Big Les, Rich bucked two shots that tore into the man's chest plate giving him two good reasons why his decision was a bad one. He never got to get off a shot. If anyone had it on their mind to buck, it was easily changed by their colleague's sudden death.

"Does anybody else need convincin' that this is not a drill, it's the real deal?" Rich asked.

He saw everyone's head shaking, indicating they understood.

"Everybody come where I can see you." Everyone made their way over to the middle of the room. "Have a seat." Rich pointed to the ground. He pushed Big Les into the middle of the floor. "Tie 'em all up and tape their mouths.

Big Les was growing tired of Rich ordering him around. Judging by the money on the table and what he estimated to be in the duffle bags, he knew he was about to take a huge loss. In addition to that, he knew once word got out on the streets that someone had singlehandedly taken down one of his stash houses it would be just a matter of time before every petty stick-up kid in town would try him, and he couldn't afford to let that happen. Big Les began duct-taping his workers' hands behind their backs. As he got to the middle person who was one of the naked girls he had bottling for him Big Les made his move.

He had no idea Rich had already anticipated his move though. The shot shattered Big Les' spine as he reached for the gun on the coffee table. The table legs collapsed from the weight of Big Les' body as he bellied over onto it. The women screamed as the men's eyes widened with fear. With no more time to waste, Rich walked over to each person on the floor and one by one began launching bullets into their skulls. He then pushed Big Les' body to the side, gathered all the money on the table, tossed it into the duffle bags, and exited the dead body–infested room. He had no need for the drugs so he left them where they were.

On his way out, he pumped a shot into Major's head. Seeing that he only had one shot remaining Rich picked up Tiny's sawed-off shotgun and split his face in two before he made his way out the door.

That night Rich had gotten away with a hundred and sixty thousand in cash, and the incident still sat in the cold case files and among the street tales as one of the greatest unsolved mysteries in the hood.

Rich brought his mind back to the present just in time to see the mugshots of the captured young bank robbers and shook his head in disgust for a second time. "Amateurs," he said as he shut the television off and called it a night.

CHAPTER TWELVE

"The following people have legal mail," the corrections officer announced.

Teflon was listening to the news on her Walkman when she heard the officer call her name. She wasn't expecting anything, but walked over to where the officer stood and waited in line. When she was handed the white envelope, the first thing she glanced at was the return address, which read United States of America Appellate Courts. Already knowing procedure, Teflon opened the envelope, took out the letter without bothering to read it, unfolded it, and shook it out. Once she signed for it she put the letter back into the envelope, shoved it into her khakis' pocket, and resumed listening to the news. Teflon wasn't in the mood to receive anymore bad news regarding her appeal. As far as she was concerned, they could all kiss her ass.

Two hours went by before the floor officer called count time. Teflon wasted no time making her way to her sleeping quarters. In passing she crossed paths with her unit manager. Over the years she and the white lady had never seen eye to eye. Teflon felt her unit manager was intimidated by her. The two had never exchanged words, but what little they had was enough to support Teflon's claim. Teflon never broke the stare of the white lady who had been eyeing her down from the time the two had noticed each other in the hallway as their paths closed in. She knew her unit manager was on her way home because this was the time she'd normally see her floating through the halls headed toward the unit's exit.

As they reached within hearing distance of each other, Teflon noticed her unit manager fixing her mouth to say something and was surprised because they never spoke in the halls or anywhere else whenever they were in each other's company.

"Congratulations. I'll see you in the morning," she dryly remarked and kept going about her business.

Teflon had no clue what the unit manager was talking about. She chalked it up to the white lady believing in the "they all looked alike" concept, confusing her with someone else in the facility. When count time cleared, as usual, Teflon took her ritual shower. When she returned to her area she took the belt out of her khakis along with everything out her pockets to change from her sweatpants into a fresh crisp pair. As she was emptying her pockets she came across the legal mail she had received earlier. She took the envelope, and tossed it into the trash. Just as she was about to slip out of her sweats and into her khakis something drew her to the trash can. She didn't know what made her retrieve the letter but she was suddenly curious about the contents. Teflon took the letter out the envelope, unfolded it, and began to read.

Dear Ms. Jackson,

After carefully reviewing the arguments and mitigating factors of your case, it is in the Appellate Courts of the United States Of America's decision to find the charges you were trialed and convicted on unwarranted and grant you immediate release.

Sincerely,
Senior Judge of Appeals
James A. Andrews

Teflon reread the letter for a second time before her brain could comprehend the words on the paper. Her eyes wanted to believe it, but she felt they were being deceived. By the time she had read the letter for a third time the words from her unit manager registered in her head and Teflon realized the white lady in fact had the right person.

So many thoughts raced through Teflon's mind. She could not believe she had been given a second chance. That in mind, her thoughts turned to Rich. She knew he was the only one who could make this possible. For years he had been promising her he would get her home. She never wanted to entertain the idea nor did she believe him, but at that moment he had turned her into a believer. She tucked the letter and speedily dressed. She couldn't wait to make her way to the telephone to share the good news with the only person she could.

The next day Teflon signed her release papers and walked out the female federal prison with nothing but a box full of letters that Rich had written to her along with her completed manuscript in a laundry bag tossed over her shoulder. Everything else she left in her locker and let all the women in her area know they could have what they pleased. She had no friends, so there was no one in particular to leave anything to. When she had spoken to Rich to share the letter with him he already knew she was coming home. He had filled her in on how the Muslim attorney he had hired contacted him the day before, informing him of the court's judgment. He told Teflon she'd be released the next day and he'd be out front waiting on her when the doors opened.

As promised, when she walked out there he was. There was no mistaking who he was when she first laid eyes on him. With the exception of the age factor, Treacherous was the spitting image of Rich. Even the way he was seated on the Harley Davidson bike instantly reminded her of Treacherous. She remembered how he had shared with her how his father had a love and passion for motorcycles. She saw Rich raise off the bike as she made her way over to him.

"What's up, ole man?" she said with a smile.

She was met with a bear hug. "What's goin' on, daughter-in-law?"

Teflon was caught by surprise by Rich's hug, but it was needed. She hadn't been embraced in a long time, and it felt good to genuinely be hugged by a loved one. She hugged him back.

"Let's get the fuck outta here," she said.

Rich released his hold. "My thoughts exactly," he replied.

"Let me drive," Teflon requested.

"It's been a long time. You sure?" Rich asked with a smile.

"Of course. Once a rider, always a rider," she replied.

Rich extended his hand, "After you then."

Teflon passed him her bag and hopped on the Harley. She turned the key in the ignition, grabbed the clutch, and started the powerful machine. The bike roared like the king of the jungle. The sound was like music to her ears.

"Come on, ole man. Whatchu waitin' for?" Teflon yelled over the bike as she revved the engine. Rich grinned and hopped on the back. Teflon came out of first gear as if she had just ridden yesterday, and within seconds Danbury Female Federal Correctional Institution became a thing of the past.

CHAPTER THIRTEEN

Rich guided Teflon to the back of the house. As soon as he'd gotten word that she was coming home, Rich went out and gathered as much as he could to make the back part of the house as cozy and comfortable as possible for her. He purchased her a brand-new mahogany-and-gold queen-size bedroom set, a thirty-six-inch flat-screen TV, a DVD/CD stereo system, and air conditioner all to be delivered. He then went to Bed, Bath, & Beyond and snatched up a comforter set, throw, with curtains to match, and extra pillows. Once he purchased that he went over to Target and picked her up any and all products he thought a woman might need. He felt kind of weird shopping for the items, especially when he caught occasional glances and looks from female shoppers. He was even tempted to buy her female undergarments, but he had no idea as to the size she wore and thought it to be inappropriate. Instead he picked her up a pack of wife beaters and boxer briefs. Once he had everything inside the room he began to put it together as best he could. When Teflon walked through the door, she was both surprised and impressed. She had no idea what to expect, but she never expected all of what she laid her eyes on. The room was immaculate. She could tell everything was brand new by the fresh smell of newness in the air. Rich had everything laid out nice and neat for her. She smiled when she saw the pack of wife beaters and boxer briefs lying on the bed next to the towel and washcloth.

"How'd you know?" she asked actually glad he had chosen them over traditional bras and panties for her.

He just grinned. "I'll leave you alone to get situated. Hope I got you everything you needed."

"You did good," she said, as she gave him a sincere hug.

"I'll be downstairs," he replied, and with that, Rich was out the door.

Teflon had been soaking for nearly an hour in the hot bath. The realization of being home had just begun to marinate as she felt the products Rich had brought for her cleansing her flesh. She stood and drained the tub. Then she turned on the shower and rinsed the remainder of the prison residue off her body. As the shower water cascaded down her back, she held her head underneath the water, placed two fingers on her clit and traveled back in time when she and Treacherous pulled a caper and had a close call. They celebrated their ability to escape by fucking like they'd never fucked before.

She remembered how Treacherous continually paced the small hotel room while she sat on the bed counting the money and observing him. It was their first bank heist and Treacherous had everything planned to a T. He had been following the bank personnel for weeks and had the bank managers routine down to a science, Mr. Brown the old security guard, name of the tellers, who took smoke breaks, who had a tendency to come to work late, who took long lunch breaks, the time the cops circled for surveillance, along with the building architecture and security system. Treacherous left no stone unturned. Nonetheless, they hadn't counted on the District Manager paying a visit to the bank that day or Mr. Brown taking ill. In Mr. Brown's absence, an off duty police officer covered his shift. That's where things got tricky. When they first noticed the changes, Teflon questioned Treacherous and suggested they hold off until another day. However, Treacherous was never one to back down from a challenge and they continued as planned. Unfortunately, the off duty police officer was gunned down along with one of the feisty tellers who decided to play hero when Teflon turned her back for a moment. The teller used the split second to press the alarm to alert the police, but Teflon caught her in action. The teller had to be used as an example to anyone else who may have wanted to test them again.

In their original plan they had twelve minutes to be in and out. Five-O made their rounds every fifteen minutes visiting two other banks along the way. This particular bank was the smallest of the three and drew the least amount of attention, but it also had the most antiquated alarm system. However, once the alarm went off, they only had half the time. Therefore, the feisty teller had to pay with her life for foiling their plans. In the end they had bodied two people and managed to get away with cash in tow. They had narrowly escaped, dumping the Kawasaki Ninja and hotwired a non-descript Buick LeSabre.

Teflon had completed counting the money. This was their biggest come up yet as she lay the stacks on the bed side by side. They had bagged nearly one-hundred and twenty-seven thousand dollars. It usually took them two-three jobs to bag that type of paper.

Treacherous was tense as he prowled the room like a caged lion, every sound, every noise outside the door had him ready to pounce. He switched the 9 from hand to hand as he looked out the window muttering to himself about tight how shit got and how the cops were probably on their ass. She knew that they had gotten away but he would be like this all night unless she literally took matters into her own hands.

Teflon pulled off her black tank top and leaned back on the bed to reveal just a tight see through bra, her nipples hardening against the sheer fabric as she undid her pants and in one swift motion pulled them off and tossed them to the floor.

She then looked at Treacherous as he stared out the window for the hundredth time. She said nothing as she slid her finger into her mouth and slowly slid it from her mouth, past her tits and finally to its intended destination on her now pulsating clit.

A slight moan escaped her lips as she gently touched her clit with *her middle finger. She closed her eyes and moved her finger down into her moist pussy and inserted it deep inside herself while raising her hips off the bed. She slid the finger out and across her clit and while the finger was still wet she moved it to her mouth tasting her own juices.*

"Hey Tef, what the fuck are you doing? We probably got the cops on our asses and you over there fuckin' around."

Teflon's first reaction was to respond but her fingers felt so good and she knew if she kept this up it would only make Treacherous angrier and he fucked good and hard when he was angry. So she kept her fingers on her clit and with her free hand she pulled down the cup of her bra to expose her hard nipple and began to play with herself.

"You fuckin' trippin'. The cops can come rollin' in the door right now and all you can think about is fuckin' getting off."

Teflon could tell he was still angry but she could also tell by the lack of pacing and his stillness that he was watching her. Now she knew she had to put on a show and really give him something to watch. She reached over and grabbed a handful of hundreds and began rubbing them on her body slowly and lustily making sure not an inch of her exposed flesh was missed. She then took some more money and placed it between her legs and began using it to rub her clit but this time in an exaggerated way and rolling her hips as she had seen the girls do in the strip clubs that she and Treacherous had parlayed at when they were looking for an easy mark.

"Baby, I'm sorry for being bad, but I'm just counting the money like you told me to" taking the hundred dollars that she had just rubbed on her clit she placed it on the bed next to her.

"One" and then taking another off her stomach she rubbed it on her pussy and moaned loudly and with purpose.

Ohhh baby, that's two..."

Teflon kept this up as Treacherous sat on the edge of the motel desk looking at her go through about six hundred dollar bills. The thought of him watching her turned her on but the feeling of him fucking her was what she really wanted.

"Baby, I can't count no more I too distracted"

"Distracted by what Tef?"

"Distracted by you standing there and knowing that you got all that dick over there and I want it nowww," she whined as she kept rubbing her self as the sound of her wet pussy was now the loudest thing in the room. She was using both hands now, right rubbing herself and her left middle and ring finger going in and out of her wetness at a furious pace.

"You look like you doing good by yourself. I guess you don't need any of this," Treacherous said grabbing his hardening manhood through his black jeans as a tease to Teflon. He was now participating in their little game.

"OHHH baby, please fuck me now...I need you in me so badly."

Treacherous rose from the edge of the desk and took off his shirt to reveal his muscular body and then slowly undid his belt and pulled it off. Now he held the belt in his hand. He then looped it through and rushed over to Teflon and snatched her hand off of her throbbing pussy. He tied her hands together and tied them over her head onto the bed post.

"You forgot the first rule, Tef...no one gets to play with the pussy unless I say its ok and that includes you..."Then he pulled the belt even harder so that there was little chance for Teflon to escape.

"OH SHIT," Tef thought but she said nothing as she waited to see what Treacherous had in mind for her next.

Treacherous pulled off his jeans and there was no doubt in Teflon's mind that she was about to get fucked. He was fully erect and it seemed like every part of him was taut and glistening including his love muscle.

Treacherous climbed on the bed and in one swft motion swiped the money off the bed. He looked at Teflon with a combination of love, lust and admiration.

"Is this what you want?"he asked as he spread her legs far apart and positioned himself right between her thighs. He then lifted her to him by grabbing her legs and pulling her hips to him, his dick inches *away from entering her wet pussy.*

Teflon's arms were tied above her head, but she wanted to hold him, she wanted to caress his strong shoulders and touch his chest but she was bound at his insistence and she knew he was about to fuck her hard.

Treacherous said nothing, he just looked at her and before she knew it he was deep inside her and she felt his dick throbbing as she reflexively lifted herself up to meet his thrust.

"Damn baby, you hit my spot every time. Don't stop, please don't stop," she begged.

Treacherous held onto her as he kept up his steady stroke, using every third or fourth stroke to go in even deeper and to make her moan even louder.

Teflon felt the swirl of passion build up inside her as her head started to spin and her pussy throbbed and grabbed even tighter to Treacherous' huge dick.

"Fuck me, fuck me harder...fuck me...I am almost there..." Teflon shouted, moaned screamed and barely got out all at once.

However, Treacherous never let up his pace or his stroke. By now he knew Teflon's pussy even better than she did. He knew that if he continued fucking her the way he was, she'd come hard as hell.

As they both grew closer, the only sound to be heard in the room was the creaking of the bed and the heavy breathing of Treacherous and Teflon as he fucked her pussy.

Oh Shit, Oh fuck. She thought, he is gonna make me cum hard and I can't do shit about it.She tried to wiggle her hands out of the belt but nothing seemed to help. She so wanted to grab Treacherous and hold him and kiss him but being tied up she could do nothing at all. She felt helpless as Treacherous worked her pussy over like the champion fucker he was.

She looked up to see his chest hovering over her as his stroke got more intense and she could barely contain herself, so she lifted up her mouth and bit him right on his pec.

"Oh shit" Teflon heard Treacherous say, "so you wanna fucking

play?" and he lifted her legs farther back and proceeded to pound deep into her pussy. His dick went so deep into her she thought he was gonna hit a vital organ but now there was no stopping him.He pushed and pounded his way into her and she knew with just a few more strokes she'd cum harder than she had ever cum before.

But she also knew Treacherous was ready she could feel him throbbing more and his stroke had become more intense and rhythmic. She really wanted them to cum together.

She started moaning, "Hurry baby, hurry...I am about to cum. Cum with me, Treach baby. Cum with me now."

Her mind exploded into a million colors and her body felt like a million little needles had touched every part of her. Teflon could feel Treacherous still stroking but it was like he was both inside her and also a million miles away. Finally, she felt him lurch and then heard him say "Fuck" and he froze on top of her. She felt him throbbing in her over and over again until he was completely spent.

He reached up and untied her arms from the bedpost and she quickly wrapped her arms around him as he laid on top of her as he had done many times before, but somehow this was different. This time it was special, because she'd seen a side of Treacherous she'd never witnessed before. This marked the beginning of their sexual exploration.

When she finally got out of the shower she put on one of her new wife beaters and boxers and pulled out a notepad. She made a to-do list and the first order of business was to find her son. She would locate him by any means necessary!

CHAPTER FOURTEEN

"I'm sorry, Ms. Jackson. This is policy. I'm only doing my job," the social worker said apologetically.

"I understand that, but why do I have to keep going through this?" she questioned, maintaining her composure. "I've completed every piece of paper that you've people asked me, and I'm still getting the run-around."

"Again, I apologize, but I'm only here today to monitor visitation, nothing more. I will say that these things take time—it's a process," she stated then cleared her throat before she spoke her next words. "And no disrespect to you, but considering your history, social services is going to be going over all of your papers with a fine-tooth comb dotting all I's and crossing all T's. That's just the way the system works."

It took all the strength she had not to reach over and grab the social worker by the throat and strangle the life out of her. She had no idea what type of history she had. Had she known the social worker would've chosen her words more carefully, Teflon told herself. Teflon had reached the point beyond frustration. She had been home for ninety days, and since then her focus had been on getting her son. When she first paid a visit to social services she was bombarded with what seemed like a ton of paperwork to fill out. Based on what little Rich had found out while she was still in prison and the caseworker, she knew Little Treacherous was being bounced around from one group home to another. It fumed her when she wasn't allowed to see him because of the requirements it took in order to be granted a visit. Rather than handling things the wrong way Teflon accepted the paper with the guidelines that would enable her to see her son. She also filled out and returned all forms to begin the process of gaining custody of her child. Now ninety days later she was being as patient as one could be in her position, waiting for someone to bring Treacherous in. She was irritated by the social worker's presence but knew for the moment this was the only way.

In her best tone, Teflon asked, "Well, how long do you estimate it would be before I'll know something?"

"Ms. Jackson, I really can't tell you that. I mean it can be six months, a year or two. It's not my decision."

Teflon couldn't believe her ears. The social worker's words tore into her heart. She knew it would be a process, but she did not think it would be as long as the social worker had just shared. She cursed the system for the way they handled things. From day one she felt the system had failed her, yet knowing that she still tried it their way. Now he it was failing her again.

"You're right it's not your decision," Teflon replied in a flat tone.

Neither the social worker nor Teflon spoke another word. The tension thickened as the silence between the two continued. Five minutes later it began to clear as both Teflon and the social worker saw two male figures approaching. Teflon stood as her son grew close. The social worker also stood.

"Thank you, Sean." She nodded to the escort and extended her hand to Treacherous. "Hello, Treacherous."

"Hi, Ms. Paterson." He shook her hand while eyeing the stranger standing next to her.

The male escort left the three of them alone.

"Do you know who this is?" the social worker asked him, seeing the expression on his face.

Treacherous shook his head.

"I'm your—"

"Ms. Jackson, please," the social worker interjected.

Had she caught the look on Teflon's face after cutting her words short her heart may have stopped. The hairs on the back of Teflon's neck were at attention. She had killed people for less, but she knew she had to keep her cool for her son's sake, but she made a mental note to remember the day.

"This is your mom," the social worker said to Treacherous.

Young Treacherous looked at Teflon, but didn't respond. Teflon wished she could read her son's mind. He took a step back and it looked like he was examining her. She was sure he had a ton of questions, but was probably being polite. She wanted to tell him that she didn't abandon him. That if she could've turned back the hands of time to be with him from day one, she would've. They had the same nose, dimples and wavy hair. He had his father's lips, eyes and rich complexion. There he stood, Treacherous, Jr., her blood. Her son.

Teflon could see his confused expression. It was a look she'd often seen on his father's face whenever he was in deep thought. There was no doubt about it, he was definitely her and Treacherous' child. She fought back her tears as she looked at him. She did not imagine she would be so emotional once she'd actually laid eyes on Treacherous Jr. At that moment all Teflon wanted to do was snatch her son up and take him home with her.

"Hey, man," she spoke.

"Hi," he replied innocently. His eyes widened and he bit into his bottom lip the way Teflon remembered doing when she was his age when she was trying to collect her thoughts.

"Treacherous, you do understand that no one's forcing you to be here. You don't have to if you don't want to," the social worker recited, doing her job.

Teflon took it harshly. She had enough of the social worker. Her patience with the lady had worn thin, and she refused to let the statement slide.

"Bitch, that's your last time cuttin' me off," she blew up. "Your ass don't have to be here either—for the rest of your life," she threatened.

Treacherous was clueless. He had no idea what had just happened.

Unbeknownst to Teflon the social worker had hit the silent alarm button on her walkie-talkie and within seconds two security guards came storming in along with the male escort who had ushered Treacherous into the room.

"Is there a problem, Ms. Paterson?" one of the security guards asked.

"Yes, Ms. Jackson was just leaving, and I need for Mr. Freeman to be escorted back to his living quarters," she calmly stated. Teflon wasn't aware of the fact that she could have gotten arrested and charged for terroristic threats..

Teflon was fighting with the decision to black out and jump on the social worker but thought better of it knowing she'd probably never gain custody of her son. She couldn't believe she had just snapped the way she had, but the social worker had pushed one too many of her buttons. She knew the lady could have made matters worse, but Teflon was not appreciative of the woman's behavior and the fact that she had the rent-a-cops breathing down her neck. She was flaming inside and knew someone would pay for how she felt dearly.

"Come on, Treacherous," the escort said, putting his arm around him.

"Bye, Mom." He waved. His words were like a fist that had just squeezed all the life out of Teflon's heart. Before she could respond Treacherous was whizzed out the room.

"Ma'am." One of the security guards reached for her.

"Don't fuckin' touch me," Teflon roared. She snatched away from the man and made her way to the door.

Rich was parked alongside Teflon's bike when she came out of the state building. He could see by the look on her face something was wrong. By the time she reached him she had just wiped her last tear.

"What's going on?" he asked.

"These muthafuckas playing games," she shouted.

"Whoa. What happened?"

"They don't wanna give me my fuckin' son, that's what happened."

Her voice echoed in the air as her words boomed out her mouth.

Rich was hoping that things would go smoothly for Teflon as she tried to gain custody of her son. When he'd first come home, aside from keeping track of where his grandson was being shipped to every time they trans-ferred him, Rich had also run into a brick wall trying to find the best way to gain custody of Treacherous. Many times he was tempted to take a different route in getting his grandson but sided against it, thinking Teflon would be able to come home and have a better chance. He realized he was wrong. He was now glad he had stuck with what he had been looking into for the past eight months, figuring he might need it for a rainy day. A thunderstorm had just hit their family, and he knew that day had now come.

"What did they say?" he wanted to know.

"Fuck what they said. I want my son, and if they don't give him to me I'mma fuckin' take him."

Rich let her words resonate. Before he said anything he first wanted to be clear on whether Teflon had meant what she just said.

"Are you sure that's what you want?"

"Rich, please don't start preachin' and shit to me. I want my fuckin' son, and I'mma get 'im by any means," she spit.

"I'm not gonna preach to you. Let's go home. We've got a lot of talking to do."

Teflon stared at him oddly. She couldn't help but notice the same look on Rich's face and tone of voice that his son had used the day he had filled her in on his thoughts, which had changed their lives forever. She didn't say anything. Instead she climbed on her R-1 as Rich started his Harley. The two of them backed out and peeled off. The whole ride home Teflon couldn't help but wonder if she had been right about what she had picked up on.

That night they talked until the sun came up. Rich had the same idea that she had, only a better way to execute it, and for the next few weeks, they went over Rich's plan until they ate, slept, and breathed it.

CHAPTER FIFTEEN

"I'm tellin' you, Troy, don't count my Cowboys out this season. Jerry Jones is gonna build Dallas back up the way we were in the nineties. I mean come on, you know football. Romo got Terell Owens and Whitten out there, not to mention Adam 'Pac-Man' Jones alongside Terrence Newman, and let's not forget Tank Johnson to clog the middle and stop the run. Hell, come to think of it, we may be better or just as good as the Troy Aikman, Michael Irvin, Emmit Smith days," Gus said. You remember when we spanked you guys," Gus ended with a chuckle.

This was a ritual for him and Troy. Today it was football, other days it was baseball or basketball. The two had been partners for nearly four years and were as different as night and day. Gus was a forty-eight years old, six feet two, 230-pound half-Irish, half-Italian ex-Marine who loved rock and roll, fast cars, fast bikes, and fast women, not to mention a love for draft beer and even more for Cuban cigars. Troy, on the other hand, was a thirty-four-year-old African-American non-drinker/nonsmoking grad student of Hampton University. He was originally from Long Island, New York, but moved to Virginia his first year in college seventeen years earlier. Standing five feet eight, weighing an even two hundred ten pounds, his rock-solid abs, compliments of his dedication to the gym and past boxing training, light skin with light brown eyes to match and wavy hair, he appeared to be a ladies' man, but he was actually a one-woman man. He had been dating the same female since his freshman year in college, had been engaged for the past six months, and just added a new addition to their lives a month ago.

It was his dream to become a homicide detective or crime scene investigator, but he somehow settled for an armed security position. When he and Gus met, despite being opposites, the two hit it off immediately due to their common interest in sports.

"Gee, why do you continue to live in the past?" Troy returned with a chuckle of his own. "Everybody knows that the New York Giants pound for pound are the best team, not only in the NFC but in the NFL."

"BBullsshitt!" Gus spit out through the phony cough in a humorous manner as he covered his mouth.

"Back at you, if you think the Cowboys are," Troy retorted.

"I never said that, my friend, but we're definitely one of them. The proof is in the pudding. Five rings, young man. How many do you guys have?" Gus questioned, already knowing the answer. "You give your New York Midgets too much credit, but it's understandable. That's how you northerners are, cocky sumsabitches."

"That's right, and we got three," Troy said proud to be from New York and a New York Giants fan.

"My point exactly. And just know, we're in a much better position to get our sixth ring before you bums get your fourth."

"Whatever," was Troy's response. He reached for the volume of the truck's radio to increase the song's sound.

"Oh no, you don't. It's my turn to pick the next song," Gus announced, reaching to change the radio's station.

"Come on, Gus. This is my jam. After this one, I promise I'll listen to whatever you want for the rest of the day."

Music was another topic the two debated throughout their four years as partners and friends. They had been on the road since 6:00 a.m. alternating their preference of music back and forth. It was now approaching 7:00 a.m. and they were due to arrive at their destination by 8:00 a.m. and nothing would make Gus more happy than to be in control of the radio for the remainder of their journey.

"Troy, you know all this hippity bee bop gives me a headache, but I tolerate it," Gus replied. To those who didn't know him, one might be offended by Gus's comments, but Troy knew his partner meant no harm or disrespect.

"I know but just this last one. Besides, your music could cause me my job, putting me to sleep." The two shared a laugh.

"Just this last one for the entire day, right?"

"Scout's honor."

"Fine."

"Thanks, friend."

Troy nodded and recited some of the verses to the hip-hop artist Jada Kiss's song playing on the radio as Gus made his way down Highway 264 West.

"Man, check out that babe right there." Gus whistled as the motorcycle breezed pass the truck.

"Gee, you know I only have eyes for my fiancé," Troy shot back, noticing the bike was occupied by a woman.

"Not the babe on the bike, knucklehead. I'm talking about the bike. She's a beaut," Gus clarified, admiring the machine.

"I knew that, just messing with you," Troy said, hoping Gus hadn't caught his embarrassment for thinking the obvious. He knew how much Gus loved motorcycles.

"She's riding that son of a gun. That's one of those R-1's right there. A lot of power in that sucker, kiddo, and see those chrome pipes, the best money can buy. She could come through an area and make that bike roar like the king of the jungle, doing about a hundred with ease right now."

"Is it faster then your Harley?" Troy asked already knowing the answer but wanting to show interest in his partner's love for bikes.

"Not in this lifetime."

Troy smiled.

Just then another bike blew past Gus and Troy on the right shoulder, passing both them and eventually the female.

"Now that's what I'm talking about," Gus roared.

"And that, my young friend, is what I'm talking about. That's a Boss Hog right there—my kind of bike, music to my ears." Gus gloated at the sight of the Harley Davidson motorcycle that was no longer in view.

"Look at them go," he continued to admire the vanished motorcycles.

Ten minutes had gone by before Gus noticed the back of the female's motorcycle in view up ahead, but the Harley was nowhere to be found. He knew she had to have made a pit stop if he was able to catch up to the powerful bike.

"There goes your baby again," Troy joked. They were just a few miles away from their intended exit before Troy dozed off. As the miles closed in, so did the motorcycles.

"A nice morning like this and all of this open road. If I were her I'd be opening that bad boy up," Gus commented to no one in particular on the fact the bike was just cruising.

"Here we are," he then said to himself since Troy was sound asleep, seeing the exit only a thousand feet or so away. The right turn signal of the motorcycle lit up, and Gus instantly caught it. Being a fellow rider, he slowed for the bike to cross over seeing they were getting off on the same exit but apparently the female rider hadn't noticed. She continued to ride in the left lane as they approached the exit. After the failed attempt, Gus accelerated to get off the exit. The bike made an attempt to exit also.

"Holy shit!" Gus shouted as the unexpected happened.

Teflon could not have timed and executed her next move any more perfectly than she had. She and Rich had gone over this countless of times. She could see the driver of the truck courteously signaling for her to exit first. She intentionally disregarded his gesture. Seeing that he had given up, Teflon watched as he sped up to get out of her way so she too could exit. She also sped up, hooking a sharp right, just inches from missing the turn. Had she not gunned it as much as she had the truck would have knocked her into the right divider, but Gus was an excellent driver and was able to come to a screeching halt. The first thing he saw when he stopped was Teflon losing control of the motorcycle and going down on the exit ramp.

"What in the hell?" Troy questioned, waking out of his slight stupor, compliments of Gus's foot slamming on the brakes.

"The crazy broad on the bike almost missed the exit and tried to make it," Gus shouted already unfastening his seat belt.

"No, I'll go and check on her. You call it in," Troy suggested unhooking his seatbelt and reaching for his issued weapon out of the glove compartment.

"Just stay here. I've got it," Gus insisted, hand already on the handle of the driver door.

"Okay. You want me to call it in?"

"Hold off. We may need to call an ambulance first if she's hurt, or she may just have the wind knocked out of her. Believe me I know. I'll let you know," he said as he hopped out of the truck. Gus made a beeline over to where the fallen female lay. It dawned on him that he had left his weapon back in the truck. His first thought was to double back and retrieve it, but he shook off the notion as he was just feet from the female and her bike. Troy watched as his partner made his way to the motorcycle.

Teflon lay still on the pavement as the drivers approached.

"Ma'am?" His voice let her know he was close by.

"Ma'am, can you hear me?" Gus kneeled down. "Ma'am, can you?" Gus attempted to repeat only to have his next words cut short.

The three shots from the silencer pierced his flesh and lodged into his lower abdomen just under his bulletproof vest. Gus never had time to think or had a chance to regret stepping out of the armored truck to aid the female without his weapon as a fourth shot followed, ripping into his skull as death greeted him.

Troy sat impatiently glancing at his watch wondering what was taking his partner so long. They were indeed behind schedule, and that was unlike his partner. Something wasn't right, Troy thought. He could feel it. Unable to wait any longer Troy honked the horn. Already they were in violation by stopping, according to policy. On top of that they hadn't called the stop in. Noticing that Gus continued to kneel hovered over the female rider and was not responsive to the sound of the horn, Troy opened the passenger door and stood on the runningboard.

"Gus," he called out. "Gus, aagh!"

Like Teflon, Rich carried out his part of the plan to a tee. It couldn't have gone any better than he had envisioned a thousand times. He had done his homework on the white security guard enough to know that Teflon's accident would cause his plan to unfold the way it was at the moment. What little he had found out about the younger of the duo was enough to

convince Rich he was the least their worries. Even now, seeing his care-
lessness by opening the armored truck's door was only confirmation in Rich's
eyes that the caper would go as smoothly as he intended.

Teflon's diversion had done the trick, Rich thought as he crept up from
the side and scaled the armored truck. Just as the door opened, Rich saw
part of the black security guard's body exposed and immediately sprang
into action. The penetration and heat of the first shot of Rich's infamous .38
revolvers caused Troy to scream out in agony as it shattered his hip bone,
causing him to lose balance in the doorway of the armored truck. As Troy
fell onto the highway's pavement, Rich hovered over him.

At the sound of Rich's weapon, Teflon released her hold on the white
security guard whom she had been firmly holding to prevent him from falling back and alarming his partner of danger. She was grateful for all the
working out she had done while in prison for had it not been for the physical
strength she had built while incarcerated she didn't think she would have
been able to hold him up as long as she had. She then slid herself from under
her bike, raised up, lifted her motorcycle onto its kick stand and stepped
over the lifeless body. As an extra precaution and confirmation, Teflon dumped
two more slugs into the slain security guard's melon before locating and
retrieving the keys to the armored truck then made her way over to the
vehicle. She checked her watch, which was synchronized with Rich's stopwatch. They were right on schedule according to the time that had elapsed
since her staged fall.

Troy lay helplessly wondering what had just happened. Furthermore,
where was his partner? All types of thoughts were racing through Troy's
mind as tears literally poured out of his eyes, soiling his face. Each time he
tried to open his eyes he was met with a blur. All he could see was his life
flashing before him, and he thought this was not the way he wanted die. His
thoughts were interrupted by the sound of voices.

"We need to get a move on things," Teflon stated. Despite for the most
part being calm, she couldn't help but to be somewhat antsy—not out of
fear but out of familiarity. Since Rich had lain down what they had to do and
what was expected of her, it had Teflon revisiting the last time she had to
ride for a man she had loved and would lay her life on the line for. Never in
a million years would she have thought she would find herself in a similar

type of predicament that could cost her her freedom, again. The ride or die chick in her convinced Teflon this time was gonna be different for a different cause.

"Absolutely," Rich agreed. "Soon as I finish this." He pointed his guns at the security guard's body.

Hearing those words sent an indescribable feeling throughout Troy's entire body. It was evident the female rider was part of the setup, just as it was apparent that his partner was dead. As if on cue his eyes popped opened and his vision became clear as his survival instincts kicked in. The first thing he saw was Rich towering over him with two revolvers in hand pointed at him.

"Please, man, don't kill me!" Troy screamed, raising his hands to prevent shots intended for his face. "Please, I'm begging you. I have a family—a wife and little boy," he offered for sympathy. His words were disregarded though.

"You should've thought about that before you chose this profession, youngin," Rich responded as he raised his two revolvers and emptied them into the upper and lower parts of the security guard. Slugs riddled Troy's body.

Not wasting any more time, Rich checked his watch and made his way to the back of the armored truck.

By the time he reached the back Teflon had already transferred a great deal of cash from two of the money bags into her duffle bag and was working on a third one.

"Only take as much as you can handle," Rich suggested.

Teflon paused and looked back at him. For a minute she thought she was looking at Treacherous. The resemblance was now stronger than ever, and there was no doubt in her mind that his words would have and could have come out of his son's own mouth had he been the one with whom she was doing the job.

"Relax. You keep forgetting, ole man, you're not the only one who worked out in the joint. Take your own advice and try not to hurt your back," she told Rich as she continued to stuff her bag with money. Now was not the time for back-and-forth, Rich knew. He shook his head, chuckled, and made a mental note to finish at a later date when this was all over with. After all, this was what their relationship had been built on. Rich dove right in, pulling his duffle bag out and following suit. Teflon glanced at her watch once again. "We gotta go," she informed Rich. "The clock is ticking."

Rich looked at his own watch. In total, sixteen minutes and twenty-two seconds had gone by. They were still eight minutes and thirty-eight seconds ahead of schedule. Although he was fully prepared, Rich was grateful no other vehicles had attempted to exit the ramp. He didn't want any more casualties than there had to be, but no one was exempt, he reasoned, if they walked into the line of fire.

"Okay, you go ahead, I'll meet you," he told her.

"See you there." Teflon slid the duffle bag full of money to the edge of the armored truck then hopped out and turned facing backward. Once she had the bags' straps over her shoulders she made her way to her R1. Rich hurried to fill his duffle bag, zipped it up then did as Teflon had with hers. So far, so good, he thought, commending himself for putting together and executing such a fool-proof plan. As he walked from around the armored truck intending to head for his Harley he saw Teflon straddling her bike. Satisfied that she was safe, Rich began to head for his own bike but something stopped him in his tracks. Something he never anticipated.

As Teflon started her motorcycle she thought she'd heard something other than the bike's engine and swung around toward the sudden noise. Reflexively, upon turning around her question was answered as she locked in on the unthinkable.

"Rich!" she cried as she snatched off her helmet, slithered her arms out of the duffle bag straps in lightning speed, and drew her weapon.

Rich never saw the bullet that pierced the left side of his neck and traveled downward finding a resting place near his chest. The impact of the shot slightly spun him around and planted him up against the armored truck. More surprised than anything, his eyes were opened wide enough to see the second shot spiraling in midair toward him. He neither had the time or the strength to reach for his AR-15, which was strapped across his chest. His mind and body fought for supremacy as one alerted him of the danger approaching, advising him to stand clear while the other resisted keeping him at a stand still.

As the second shot plunged into his upper torso, Rich could hear Teflon's cries in the distance. He knew it was just a matter of time before she made her way over to him. He was actually more concerned with her well-being than his own. The last thing he wanted to see was their plans go in vain. He couldn't believe he had been caught slipping. There was no doubt in his mind that his final fate would be handed down to him on the exit of the interstate. He had told himself when he was released from prison that returning was not an option. Rich never thought this would be the way he would breathe his last breath, but this was the life he had chosen for himself, and he was content with what came behind it. He and his shooter made eye contact just before the third bullet was released.

The shooter's face was bloodied and unrecognizable from the previous shots he had endured. Rich couldn't help but respect the man's will to live and serve out his duty, but he didn't regret what he had done to him. The only regret Rich had was that he hadn't finished the security guard off. Rich could hear the sounds of other shots in the distance and knew the only place they could be coming from.

Troy's head was spinning. He had just regained consciousness as he lay there fighting for his life. Images of his wife to be and son paraded in his mind. It was those images that kept him holding on. Troy had felt each bullet pierce his flesh and knew he had been hit numerous times, so he wasn't sure if he would make it. All he could think about was staying alive long enough for him to see his family one more time. Despite his body being filled with at least a half-dozen slugs, Troy felt a discomfort on his right side. Something was poking him and he knew what that something was. Troy strained to shift his body and lifted his left arm to retrieve the weapon from underneath him. He remembered how he had placed it on his hip when he and Gus had stopped for the female's fake fall. He somehow managed to get his body to slightly shift just enough to reach his service weapon, but the weight of his arm felt like a ton each time he tried to raise it. Tears trickled out the corners of his eyes from the excruciating pain, but still he refused to give up. He attempted to raise his arm for the fifth time. A sharp pain jolted his body as he raised it again just below his side. It seemed to be getting heavier and heavier with each strain.

"You caaan dooo it." Troy grunted as he exerted all the strength he had into the attempt. It was enough to get his arm onto his chest. Accomplishing that, an out-of-breath Troy inched his hand toward the weapon. A sense of achievement mixed with relief filled him as he felt his fingertips brush the butt of his weapon. Having his left arm over his chest made it easier for Troy to shift his body even more. He knew his next move was going to be crucial and had to be precise. All in one motion, Troy threw all his weight to his right side and slid his hand onto his weapon. As he felt himself rolling over he was able to lock in on the weapon and pull it out before he landed on his stomach. Still out of breath, Troy let out a few blood-filled coughs. Just then he heard sounds coming from the back of the armored truck. He hoped the perpetrators hadn't heard him. Troy's adrenaline was pumping. With what little strength he still possessed, Troy was able to release his safety on his forty cal and aimed it in front of him, prepared for whoever or whatever came from behind the armored truck. Seconds turned into minutes without anyone coming, but Troy continued to play possum, laying there waiting patiently on the ground for any opportunity that presented itself.

Just then Troy heard footsteps and knew it was either now or never. He focused his aim on the end of the armored truck and locked in. He knew he'd have to act fast and make his shots count. With each footstep Troy's heart rate increased, but no one appeared around the corner. The sound of the motorcycle's engine behind him startled Troy, nearly causing his heart to leap out his chest, but not enough to cause him to lose focus on his aim. Fortunately for Troy he was able to maintain his composure. He would have never seen the robber before the robber had seen him as he came from around the side of the armored truck. Troy's right blood-stained eye grew small as it locked in on its intended target, and without hesitation he fired a round. By the way the robber's body slammed up against the vehicle Troy knew his shot was successful.

His second round was fired with confidence, finding its intended target once more. Troy's eyes met with the man who was responsible for him laying there on the ground. Although his seemed much darker and cold, Troy could see pain in his assailant's eyes and wondered if the man had seen that same pain in his own. He didn't care that he was another black man like himself and didn't care that he had a family waiting for him at home. And with that thought in mind Troy squeezed the trigger and released a third shot, but never got to see its final destination. The last thing Troy heard was a woman's voice.

Teflon got off her bike with her gun in hand, racing toward the direction of the sudden commotion. The first thing she spotted was Rich planted up against the side of the armored truck. Instantly she flew into a blind rage. She had just reached the security guard laid on the ground as he fired his next shot.

"Muthafucka!" Teflon screamed, and without thinking twice, she pumped three shots into the back of his head. She then rushed over to Rich.

Rich watched in admiration as Teflon finished off the security guard and came to his aid. If he ever had any doubt, which he hadn't, there was no room for any now as to why his son had loved her so much. At that moment, Rich deemed Teflon the true definition of a ride or die chick.

"Shit," Teflon cursed, seeing the blood seeping out the side of Rich's neck. "Give me your hand." She placed Rich's hand on the side of his neck and pressed it against it. "Just hold that right there 'til I find something." She examined Rich's body for other wounds. "Where else are you hit?"

In an attempt to make light of the situation, Rich cracked a smile. "Don't worry about me, baby girl. I'll be alright. You need to get out of here," he said calmly.

"What?"

"You heard me. You gotta go. You gotta stick to the plan."

"I see these fuckin' bullets got you delirious," Teflon said, ignoring his suggestion. "If you gonna talk stupid, don't talk at all. Save your strength."

"Hold on, youngin. I'm still your elder," Rich shot back.

"And you're also my partner, so act like it," Teflon shot right back. "We're in this together—ride or die, right?"

Rich could not dispute that. That was the creed they lived by. "He caught me under here," he offered, indicating he had been hit in the upper torso.

"I gotta get you outta here." Teflon knew the only way Rich could have any chance of living was if she got him somewhere where she could nurse and dress his wounds. She also knew she could not handle the one duffle bag let alone two and Rich all on her bike. Her mind was operating at two hundred miles per hour, trying to figure out the best way to handle the situation. Just then an answer appeared.

***

A tired Judy Smith had been driving for the past three-and-half hours since 4:00 a.m. from Washington, DC, and she was relieved to see her exit up ahead. Although she was tired, she was not in the least bit complaining. After all, this was the opportunity she had been waiting for. Being a thirty-two-year-old white female who had been working in a corporation run by men since she was the ripe age of twenty-one, she jumped at the chance to represent the firm, Trinity Communications and be privy to the next promotion. Her navigation system said she was only eight miles away from her final destination. Her business meeting was scheduled for 9:30 a.m., which gave her more than enough time to check into the hotel and make it to her meeting on time. "In three hundred feet, exit right," the navigation system announced.

Judy put her turn signal on and veered over toward the exit.

"Fuck," she cursed under her breath seeing that traffic was backed up on her exit. She slowed the Dodge Avenger down twenty feet from the back of the armored truck.

Judy impatiently checked her Rolex watch. "Come on, people," she yelled to no one in particular. Just then a woman appeared from the side of the armored truck heading in Judy's direction. There was no doubt in her mind now that an accident had occurred up ahead. Judy rolled down her driver's side window to find out what was going on.

"Good morning."

That was all she was able to get out before Teflon drew her gun from behind her back and shoved the nine millimeter in the car, dumping one shot in her skull. Part of Judy's brain matter splashed across the passenger's window as she slumped over the steering wheel. Teflon immediately sprang into action. She opened the driver's side door and unfastened the seat belt then grabbed the woman by the back of the neck, snatched her up, and flung her out of the car. She checked the time. They were twelve minutes behind schedule with eighteen minutes remaining before the armored truck's dropoff would become suspicious and investigate. Teflon dragged the woman's body to the armored truck, reopened the back, picked her up, and tossed her inside.

"You still with me?" she asked Rich who had slid to the ground.

"Yeah, barely," was his response.

"What's important is that you're still here. We don't have much time. I found us a way outta here," Teflon informed Rich.

"Yeah, I heard." He grinned in reference to the shot he'd heard moments ago.

"By any means necessary, right?" Teflon stated.

"By any means necessary," he repeated.

"I need you to lift up so I can take this bag to the car," she told Rich, leaning over him. Once she assisted him in freeing his arms from the duffle bag, Teflon hiked the bag over her shoulder and lugged it to the car. She reached inside the Dodge Avenger and popped the trunk then threw the duffle bag inside before making her way to retrieve the one she had laid beside her bike. Once both bags were secured Teflon hurried back over to Rich.

"Come on, ole man. Lets get you outta here," Teflon said as she reached down to help Rich from the ground.

"What I tell you about all of that ole man nonsense? Ain't nothing ole about me but my soul."

"Yeah, yeah, you can tell me all about it later. Right now let me get you to this car," Teflon told him.

Rich noticed the unlucky person's brain matter plastered all over the passenger's side window as soon as Teflon opened the door.

"You gotta wipe that off before we go. Can't be riding around like this," Rich advised right before she secured him in the car.

"I know."

Teflon took off her black leather riding jacket then took her black "I Ride Hard" t-shirt off and began wiping the window. Satisfied she had gotten the bulk of the brain debris off she balled up the t-shirt. "Here, put this on your neck." She threw her jacket inside the car, closed the door, and made her way to the driver's side.

She started the car and again took a look at her watch. Three seconds after she looked at it, the alarm sounded on both hers and Rich's indicating they had reached the time they had given themselves for the caper they had just pulled. They were supposed to have been long gone, but the unexpected had happened, just as it had when she and Treacherous had pulled their last caper together. Too many similarities, Teflon thought, but she refused to let the final outcome end the same. She threw the Avenger in reverse and backed off the ramp then back onto the highway. She knew there was no way for authorities to trace the motorcycles back to them because they were stolen, so she had no problem leaving them on the ramp's exit. Teflon put the car in drive and accelerated onto the highway headed for the next exit. Just as she sped off a car was slowing to exit. She counted her blessings for making it off the ramp in time and onto the highway unnoticed.

"Recalculating," the navigation system wailed out of nowhere. Teflon took the butt of her weapon and smashed the system until it went silent.

"You killing up everything today, huh?" Rich said humorously in a raspy tone still applying pressure to his gunshot wound.

"I swear you and your son should've been twins." She laughed.

"No, you and him should have been brother and sister." The two of them both shared a laugh.

In record-breaking time, Teflon closed in on the exit, which was seven miles from where they had just departed.

"I'm gonna stop and take care of you then come back as soon as I get Li'l Treach," Teflon suggested.

"Like hell you will," Rich said. "I'm good. Remember, we're in this together, ride or die."

"But—"

"But nothing. Let's stick to the script and go get my grandson." Rich took charge despite his condition. Teflon didn't argue with him. Instead, she exited off the highway and headed for their next destination.

CHAPTER SIXTEEN

"Charlie One, this is Charlie Two," the helicopter radioed in.

"Go ahead, Charlie Two."

"I have a visual on the location."

"Copy that, Charlie Two. What's the status?"

"We have two bodies, an armored car, two motorcycles, another vehicle, and a pedestrian on foot on Exit 87 on Interstate 264. Requesting all available units to location."

"Copy that, Charlie Two."

The helicopter watched as the pedestrian continued to jump up and down, waving his arms in the air in an attempt to flag him down. Unable to land and assist in whatever had taken place on the ramp, the helicopter hovered over the area until backup arrived on the scene. Within minutes, all available units swarmed the surrounding area.

"Jesus freakin' Christ, what took you guys so freakin' long?" a twenty-six-year-old Caucasian man name Todd ranted to the first officer to arrive, walking toward the patrol car as soon as the officer stepped out. "There's freakin' bodies all over the place."

Instantly he was met with a gun pointed in his direction. "Sir, stay where you, and let me see your hands," the trooper shouted.

"Holy shit," Todd nervously yelled, complying with the orders. "Dude, you got the wrong guy."

"On your knees now," another trooper yelled with his gun drawn as well.

"This is bullshit," Todd bellowed. "I called you fuckin' guys." He dropped to his knees. In seconds, Todd was surrounded by what seemed to be a hundred police.

The first officer on the scene placed handcuffs on him.

"What's your name?"

"I didn't do any fuckin' thing," he responded.

"Sir, what is your name?" the officer repeated.

"Todd Anderson."

"Mr. Anderson, you have the right to remain silent."

Just then a shift commander arrived on the scene. "Who do we have here?" he asked the officer.

"He claims his name is Mr. Todd Anderson," the officer said slamming the suspect against the car.

"You said, a Mr. Anderson?" he questioned lifting his shades to get a better look at the perp.

"Yeah, chief."

"Take those handcuffs off him," he ordered.

An I-told-you-so look appeared on Todd's face when the trooper uncuffed him.

The trooper paid him no mind. He had seen worse looks and had been cursed out enough in similar situations and had become immune to it.

"Thank you, chief," Todd said as if the two had known each other their entire life.

Chief Andre Randle had been in law enforcement thirty-three of his fifty-two years, choosing the profession, initially thinking he could solve the unsolved murder of his older brother who was the victim of a racial hate crime one uneventful evening after a bullet took his life while leaving a high school party. He never did crack the case, but had since then solved many others. Being African American and from the Norfolk area gave the chief an advantage over others when it came to the way he did his job. It was in fact his street smarts that contributed to his success over the years. His experience and knowledge of the urban communities earned him a ninety-eight percent crime-solving rate. Today he intended to maintain that number.

"Please come with us, Mr. Anderson," the chief replied. He waved officer Perez over to accompany them for questioning.

Todd followed as the police on the scene secured the area. Todd could see flares alongside the ramp trailing up to the top of the exit, the area being taped off and officers walking around in search of clues as to what may have happened.

"Mr. Anderson, you were the one who notified 911, correct?" the chief asked.

"That's correct."

"Can you tell us what you saw?"

"Sure. I was coming home down 264 after leaving my girlfriend Debbie's house out in Virginia Beach."

"Where's home?" the officer asked, taking notes.

"Right here. Norfolk."

"Okay. Go on."

"So, I'm driving down the highway coming up on my exit when I see this asshole, excuse this freakin' car backing up off the exit ramp, and I'm thinking to myself, this idiot is lost."

"Why would you think that?" the chief asked.

"Because the car had Washington, DC, tags on it."

"Did you happen to remember the plate number," the other officer asked.

"Not really, but the first two letters did stick out," Todd answered.

"Why is that?"

"Because they were our state's initials."

"You mean VA?"

"Yup."

"Okay, that's good. What about the car? Can you tell us the make of the car?"

"Now that I can help you with. That's easy because my aunt Sharon has one just like it, only hers is silver, and I think it's a freakin' knockoff of the Magnum and Charger, but I like the Charger best," Todd rambled.

The chief's tolerance was wearing thin. "Mr. Anderson, please just answer Officer Perez' question."

"Oh, sorry about that, sir. Yes, it was a royal blue Dodge Avenger."

"Thank you, Mr. Anderson. Is there anything else you can think of that may be of assistance to us?" the chief asked.

"Uh," he thought. "Oh, I think there were two people in the car and I could be wrong on this one but it looked like it was a woman driving, an African American woman. That's all I can think of."

"Thank you, Mr. Anderson. You've been more than helpful, and I apologize for any inconvenience this may have caused you. We just need to take all of your information in case we have additional questions. Perez, take down all of Mr. Anderson's information and then call this in," he said all in one breath to Todd and the investigating officer.

"On it."   Officer Perez hurried off.

"You're welcome, chief. Anytime, just wish I could've been more helpful. I hope you catch the bastards who did this though," Todd bellowed.

"So do I," the chief responded just as he was bombarded with more bad news.

"Chief, we got another one," the officer informed him. "In the back of the armored truck."

Todd stood there trying to being nosey, hoping to get an earful to add to the story he would tell his friends later in the day.

"Have a good day, Mr. Anderson," the chief said, dismissing Todd.

Catching the hint Todd made tracks to his vehicle.

"See to it that Mr. Anderson makes it to his vehicle and safely out of the area," the chief said to another officer.

"No problem, chief."

"What do we have?" the chief asked.

"Don't look good, chief."

"It never does. Give it to me."

"Three dead bodies. Two security—the driver forty-eight-year-old Gustoff Constanza, and the passenger thirty-four-year—old Troy Davis—both out of Norfolk. Multiple gunshot wounds to upper and lower parts of the body. We found casings near both bodies nine-millimeters near the driver, nine-millimeter and .40 caliber near the passenger. In the back of the armored, thirty-two-year-old Judy Smith of Washington, DC, one shot to the head close range. My guess is she was shot somewhere else and placed in the back of the truck."

"That answers where the car came from," the chief said.

"What car, chief?"

"The one the perps got away in. Witness said he saw a Dodge Avenger with DC plates backing off the ramp."

"That explains why we found two motorcycles."

"But why ride motorcycles then jack a car?" the chief questioned, noticing the bikes. "Why not just drive a car? Unless," he said, answering his own question. "Didn't you say there were two different shell casings near the passenger security guard?"

"Yeah."

"Have someone check his hand and weapon to see whether he fired it and have everyone check for traces of blood," the chief ordered as he put the pieces together in his head.

"On it."

Five minutes later the officer returned with the information the chief already knew existed.

"You were right as usual, chief. It's been confirmed that the security guard's .40 caliber was fired. I checked the gun myself. Out of a full clip, three bullets were missing. Judging by the way he was laying chances were he fired at something—or rather someone—in front of him, so I followed the path and it lead me right to a blood trail next to the armored truck," the officer announced, proud of himself for what he believed to be great detective work.

"Good job, sergeant. Have someone run a sample back to headquarters immediately for DNA."

"Already three steps ahead of you, chief."

"And also, have them do a printout of anyone in the seven-city area with bank robbery on their jacket, male and female, starting with the city of Norfolk first," the chief requested.

"Gotcha."

The chief placed his hands behind his back and began walking around, scanning the area for something that may leap out at him to help tell the complete story. "Come out, come out wherever you are," he chimed to himself.

CHAPTER SEVENTEEN

Meanwhile across town, Teflon was just blocks away from her intended destination.

"How you feelin' over there?" she asked Rich.

"As strong as an ox," he answered.

Teflon smiled. His answer was to be expected. "And as smart as a fox," she finished.

"Exactly."

Teflon arrived on the block of the house that social services had assigned little Treach and parked mere houses away from the address written on the piece of paper. "We're here," she informed Rich.

"Okay. You ready?"

"Most definitely, but you're not. You're in no condition. Just stay here. I'll go in, grab him, and be back as soon as I can."

"Like hell." He coughed. "I'm going."

She cut his words short. "Look at you. You're bleeding all over the place, Rich. If you go in with me like that all you're gonna do is leave an easy blood trail for them to follow. It's just a matter of time before they find it back there and run it, so we don't have time to waste. Trust me, I got this. I'm going to be in and out, and I'm not gonna let anything or anyone stand in my way of doing just that. If someone so much as blinks the wrong way I'm gonna cash their ass out. Now let me go in and get your fuckin' grandson so we can get the hell out of VA."

Rich could not argue with Teflon and he didn't have the strength to. She was one hundred percent right. He had already thought about how he had jeopardized their plan by getting caught slipping. He also knew he was in no condition to get out of the car let alone make it into the house. Each minute he felt himself getting weaker and weaker. It was his pride that caused him to continue to stand firm, but after hearing Teflon's words he reasoned with himself not to allow his ego to stand in the way of what needed to be done and how it needed to be carried out.

"Hurry up and go get my grandson," he said.

"Thank you."

Teflon checked her guns. She stuck one in the lower part of her back and shoved the other in her shoulder holster.

"Be back in a sec," she assured Rich, leaning over and planting a kiss on his forehead before exiting the Dodge Avenger.

"Alright kids, time to do your house chores and freshen up before we eat," the elderly staff lady announced.

Children ranging from six to sixteen began to scurry to their assigned areas. Most of them had been at the house long enough to incorporate the daily schedule into their daily routine. Treacherous had been at the house for nine months, the longest he had ever been at one place. In total he had been to twenty-three different spots affiliated with social services from the time he was born up until that moment. None of the others lasted longer than six months. As usual, he kept to himself and only did what he was told—nothing more, nothing less. His job was to take out the trash before and after each meal. Treacherous made his rounds, gathering up the filled garbage bags in the cans throughout the house. Retrieving three out of the five bags he then made his way toward the back of the house. Just as he reached the back door he heard the front doorbell ring.

Ms. Davis, the head of staff, stopped what she was doing and looked up at the hallway's clock on the wall. It was well after visiting hours. She walked toward the front door.

"Yes? May I help you?" she asked, opening up the front door.

"Yeah, if you don't wanna die," Teflon answered. She had already drawn her gun from behind her back. She pushed her way through the door and aimed her gun at the woman's face.

Instantly she threw up her hands. "I don't understand," she exclaimed. She was noticeable afraid for her life.

"I came for my son," Teflon announced. She scanned the house as she spoke. From what she could see all the children and the other staff were preoccupied and her sudden presence had gone unnoticed.

"Young lady, please calm down," Ms. Davis tried to reason.

"My son name is Treacherous Freeman. You have two minutes, one to locate him and the other to bring him to me without making a scene or you will not live to see another day. Are we clear?" Teflon calmly stated.

Teflon gave the woman a cold-hearted look and her tone stern and it was apparent that Teflon meant business.

"Yes," she answered. "Please follow me."

Teflon concealed her weapon and followed.

"Ms. Davis, I finished straightening up," a little girl said as Teflon and Ms. Davis walked through the house.

"Very good." Ms. Davis' voice cracked. "Now go get ready for supper."

The little girl hurried off to do as she was told. Ms. Davis nervously continued to search for Treacherous.

"Is everything okay, Ms. Davis?" one of the male staff members asked, noticing her peculiar expression.

"Yes. Everything is fine, Tyrone," she carefully replied.

"Okay. Hello," he said, addressing Teflon. She nodded and shot him an award-winning warm smile. She watched him closely to see if he was aware of any imminent danger. She could tell by the way he was staring at her that something else was on his mind other than her being a threat. Convinced he was clueless, Teflon placed her hand on Ms. Davis' shoulder. "I really need to be going," Teflon hinted.

"Of course," Ms. Davis replied, "Tyrone, have you seen Treacherous?"

Tyrone looked at his watch. "He should be out back emptying the trash," he offered.

"That's right," Ms. Davis recalled.

"He should be coming back in now," he added.

"Thank you, Tyrone."

Just then Teflon heard the familiar voice. It took everything in her power not to let the three-letter word melt her heart.

"Mom?" Treacherous called out.

He couldn't believe his eyes when he saw her standing with Ms. Davis and Mr. Waters. Even from the side view despite only meeting and seeing her once he could tell it was his mother. It was a face he had locked in and taken to bed with him every night since the first time he had laid eyes on her. Although it was good to see her, Treacherous wondered how she had found him and what she was doing there.

"Treach baby, come here," she spoke in a motherly tone.

Ms. Davis remained silent. Treacherous walked over to his mother. Teflon embraced him with her left arm and kissed him on the forehead.

"We're leaving," she told him.

Her words not only surprised Treacherous but Tyrone as well.

"Ms. Davis, what's going on?" he asked. Teflon could now see in his face that he had figured something wasn't right. Wasting no time, she sprung into action. Treacherous' eyes widened at the sight of the gun his mother drew.

"Get the fuck over there," she barked, waving the black piece of steel at both Ms. Davis and Tyrone, more so at Tyrone as she placed Treacherous behind her. The bass of her voice echoed throughout the house, alarming the other two female staff on duty and the other thirty-four children it housed.

"Everybody over here," she commanded, drawing her second weapon.

Fear filled the air as screams and cries of young children outweighed the echo of Teflon's orders.

In seconds everyone in the entire house was packed together in front of Teflon like sardines.

"As long as everyone does as I say, nobody will get hurt," Teflon announced.

Children and staff both nodded in agreement.

"How many phones are in this house?" She directed her question to Ms. Davis.

"Three," she replied.

"Where?"

"One over on the wall, another at the top of the stairs, and one in my office back there." Ms. Davis made sure to be truthful and accurate.

"Where's your first aid kit?" she asked.

"It's in my office under my desk."

"Treach, go into the kitchen and get a knife," Teflon instructed her son, "then go and cut all phone lines, get the first aid kit, and come right back, you hear me?"

"Uh-hmm." Treacherous nodded and hurried to the kitchen.

"Sister, you don't have to do this," Tyrone blurted out.

"Muthafucka, I ain't ya sistah, now shut the hell up," Teflon barked.

All the children's eyes widened at Teflon's words.

"Tyrone, please," Ms. Davis begged.

"What?" He threw his hands up. "I was only trying to help."

Teflon walked toward him. "You wanna help? Keep your fuckin' mouth shut."

Treacherous was just returning after cutting the last phone line in Ms. Davis' office when he heard his mother screaming at Mr. Waters.

"Anybody with cell phones, pull 'em out," she ordered. The two female staff in the back immediately raised their phones in the air. Ms. Davis did the same in the front, but Tyrone hesitated.

"Treach, go get those," she instructed.

"Think about what you're doing," Tyrone said making yet another attempt to reason with her. "It's not too late."

"Yes it is," she calmly said just as the bullet exited the chamber of her gun and entered Tyrone Waters' mouth. The bullet killed him instantly.

The shot caused Ms. Davis to faint and one of the female staff to vomit while all the kids and the other female staff screamed uncontrollably.

"Everybody be quiet and no one else will be hurt," Teflon assured them all.

She knew it was time to get out of the group home. She stepped over

Tyrone's body and retrieved Ms. Davis' cellular phone which had hit the ground right before she had. She then turned back to Tyrone's lifeless body and snatched his phone out of his hip clip. When she grabbed his phone Teflon could hear a voice coming from it. She looked at the screen of Tyrone Water's phone.

"Fuck," she exclaimed, seeing 911 plastered across the screen. The call showed it had been running for the past three minutes. Teflon cursed herself for not noticing Tyrone dialing the number.

"Treacherous baby, let's get up outta here," she told her son.

Treacherous made his way over to Teflon. Before she reached the front door Teflon pumped two more bullets into Tyrone's lifeless body then grabbed Treacherous' arm and hurried out the door. One of the female staff rushed to Ms. Davis as soon as she heard the front door slam.

CHAPTER EIGHTEEN

Chief Randle was just making his way back toward the armored truck when he heard his name called. He could see excitement in his sergeant's face as he approached him.

"Tell me something to make me smile," he told the sergeant.

"How about this?" the sergeant said. "We got a positive ID on the DNA we found. You ready?" the sergeant asked.

"I'm listening."

"DNA belongs to a Mr. Richard Robinson."

"Robinson?" the chief ran the name around in his head.

"Come on, chief. I was told you would recognize the name."

"Richard Robinson?" he asked still a little uncertain.

"Maybe this will refresh your memory. I did like you said and had them pull up all ex-cons who had any type of armed robbery on their jacket, male and female, starting with the ones in the local area from the biggest to the smallest, and guess what?"

"Come with it," the chief said.

"Richard Robinson's name was number two on the list. He served more than twenty-five years for armed robbery. Got caught after he got away with over a million dollars from Bank of America. Ring any bells?"

The moment the sergeant made mention of the bank's name and how long ago the case was, the bells began to burst his eardrums. Richard Robinson. Now it all made sense and it was finally coming together. It was his first time working a bank job as a detective. It was also the case that had gotten him promoted to head detective in his division.

"You've gots to be kiddin' me. I thought he was dead," the chief said nodding his head in disbelief and cracking a partial smile

"Nope. Alive and kicking. But wait, it gets better," the sergeant continued. "Do you remember about ten years ago the same bank was hit again by a young couple?"

"Now that I remember," the chief answered. "It was all over the news when I came back from vacation. I was pissed I wasn't here to work the case. I think they were calling them the modern-day Bonnie and Clyde. The goddamn boyfriend battled it out not too far from here on 264 if I remember, and the girlfriend was found unconscious in the car."

"You remember, right?" the sergeant said. "But there's something you forgot about that whole incident."

"What's that?" the chief was eager to know.

"That the boyfriend was Richard Robinson's son."

"Jesus, how could I forget?" the chief retorted.

"Wait though. When the list for the females came out, guess whose name popped up?"

The Chief knew the answer to that one. "The girlfriend."

"The girlfriend," the sergeant repeated. "Seems her federal sentence was overturned and she's been out for a few months now. May be a long shot but—"

The chief and sergeant were interrupted by one of the officers on the scene.

"Excuse me, chief. Dispatcher thought you might be interested in a 911 call that just came in. They think it may be connected to the armored truck hit." He handed the chief the walkie-talkie.

"This is Chief Randle. Go."

"Hey, chief, this is Wendy. I was forwarded this call from 911. It came in about five minutes ago. You listening?" The recording played as the chief listened intently.

"Christ" Chief Randle bellowed hearing the shot go off after an exchange. He didn't have to witness it to know the female perp had just killed the man talking. Screams of children could be heard in the background.

Chief Randle listened until the call ended, putting it together in his mind.

"Wendy, do me a favor. Play the ending back one more time for me," he requested as something leaped out at him. He wanted to be sure he had heard what he'd thought he had.

"Sure. "Everybody be quiet and no one else will be hurt."

"Fuck. Treacherous baby, let's get up outta here."

"Son of a bitch."

This time the sergeant caught it as well.

"Chief, are you thinking what I'm thinking?"

"I am but it's impossible. There's no way Treacherous Freeman could still be alive. Hell the shit was on national television, unless—" the chief said.

"Wendy, get me an address on that location ASAP."

"Already have it."

"Unless what, chief?"

"Those were kids screaming in the background, right?"

"Yeah, so," the sergeant said, still in the dark.

"So maybe Treacherous was a kid."

"Her son?"

"Exactly."

As soon as he said that, the dispatcher came back on the line. "Chief, the address is to a group home for kids. You ready?"

"Shoot," he said as the smirk appeared on his face. Once he jotted the address down, Chief Randle made a mad dash for his vehicle.

CHAPTER NINETEEN

Rich opened his eyes at the sound of the car door opening. He smiled when he saw Teflon getting in the front seat and Little Treacherous in the back. Teflon looked over at Rich to check on him.

"You good?"

He nodded.

"Treach, hand me that box."

Treacherous handed his mother the first aid kit. "We need to put something on your neck right quick." Teflon opened the box and pulled out the peroxide, gauze pads, and a gauze cloth roll. She leaned into Rich. "This may sting a bit. Man up."

Rich smiled. He braced himself and clinched his teeth as the sensation of the liquid ignited his insides. Treacherous watched from the back as his mother nursed the stranger's wound.

"Hold this," she instructed Rich placing his hand on the gauze pads. Quickly she wrapped the cloth roll around his neck. Under the circumstances she knew she had done the best she could. Once she felt she had Rich's wound sedated Teflon started the car and peeled off. The peroxide and bandages with which Teflon dressed his neck wound brought a little relief to Rich's discomfort.

Rich managed to shift and looked back at his grandson. He couldn't believe the strong resemblance to his son when Treacherous was his age. "Hey, li'l man." He spoke in a low, raspy tone.

Treacherous did not speak. He wondered who the man was who sat in the front passenger seat. Whoever he was, Treacherous could see he was bleeding. Rich's blood had soiled the side of the passenger seat.

"Say hello to your grandfather," Teflon told him.

"Hi," Treacherous kept it short.

"That's your father's dad," she explained.

Rich grinned. Treacherous noticed the grin resembled the same one he often found himself displaying at times for different reasons.

"We have plenty of time to get to know each other," Rich said to Treacherous before turning back around. "So what took so long?"

"Tsk, it got crazy in there. Some muthafucka tried to play Dr. Phil and I had to slump his dumb ass."

"So much for in and out smooth. No kids, right?"

"No kids, but this piece of shit I was tellin' you about snuck and called 911. Don't really know all they got but his phone was on for about three minutes."

Rich frowned. Hearing that, he knew it was just a matter of time before authorities got on their trail if they hadn't already.

"We gotta get out of VA right now," Rich managed to say through coughs.

"I know," Teflon agreed as she accelerated .

Chief Randle was just minutes away from the group home when the unexpected call came through.

"Chief Randle, are you there?"

"This is Chief Randle. Go."

"Just got a call saying they got a visual on that royal blue Dodge Avenger. It's heading northbound on 264 near Interstate 64. They're redirecting all available units. The news caused the chief to slam on his brakes. He threw the patrol car in reverse, backed up to the intersection's opening and made a U-turn in the middle of the highway after traveling south. The chief wasted no time darting out into the ongoing traffic. He floored the gas pedal until the speedometer read a hundred twenty.

Fifteen miles up the highway Teflon continued to gaze up at the helicopter that seemed to surface every five minutes as she navigated the car. She couldn't help but think about the last time a helicopter hovered over her on a highway, but shook off the thought.

"I keep seein' that damn helicopter." She pointed to Rich.

"Yeah me too," Rich said. He was convinced they were being followed. He had enough run-ins to know when the heat was on. He could practically feel them breathing down their necks.

"I think I should get off and switch cars," Teflon suggested.

Rich shook his head in disagreement. "If they're on us that'll be a bad move. As soon as we get off they'll be swarming us."

"If we stay in this it's gonna be the same thing. We can't outrun anything in this slow-ass muthafucka."

Rich was thinking the same thing. Still there was no time to make any type of pit stops. He looked up and saw that the copter was still in view.

"We can't stop," Rich stated.

Teflon sighed and looked back at her son. "You okay, man?"

"Um-hmm." Treacherous shook his head. He sat quietly and listened to his mother and grandfather's conversation. Little by little he was putting the pieces together as best his young mind would allow him. Although he was glad to be with his mother he still couldn't figure why she had come to get him the way she had. Whatever the case, he knew it wasn't good. Then just like that the worse appeared.

Teflon saw the state trooper patrol car alongside the road to her left. A bad feeling began to invade her.

"Just be cool," Rich said.

"I'm cool."

They both were aware troopers were posted up throughout the interstate but had hoped they could avoid a head on confrontation, but as she passed the patrol car their hopes became a distant thought that vanished into thin air.

"Damn," she cursed.

The flashing lights of the state trooper's patrol car appeared in the Avenger's rearview mirror.

Rich strained to reach down on the floor in front of him.

"Baby, put your seat belt on," Teflon instructed Treacherous. She looked over to see Rich preparing what they both knew was to come.

Rich checked his AR-15 then set it in his lap.

"Treach, reach under Mommy's seat and pass that up to me."

Treacherous unfastened his seat belt, reached under the driver's seat, and retrieved the identical replica of the weapon Rich had and handed it to his mother. Treacherous noticed a vanilla-colored envelope under his mother's seat as well.

Teflon placed her AR-15 between her and Rich, closest to her.

"Thank you, man. Now put your seat belt back on."

Treacherous did what he was told.

"You want me to stop?"

"Might as well," Rich replied. "We're all in now. Ride or die, right?"

"Ride or die."

The trooper had already unsnapped the latch of his gun holster and drew his weapon as he stepped out of his patrol car. He cautiously made his way over to the passenger side of the vehicle. Despite the report saying the suspects were armed and dangerous he sided against waiting for backup and instead approached the vehicle with his weapon pointed at the front seat.

"Ma'am, turn off the vehicle and let me see your hands, both of you" he shouted his eyes going back and forth from Teflon to Rich. Seeing that no one complied, the trooper became more aggressive with his tone. "Ma'am, turn the vehicle off now!"

Rich let off a barrage of shots through the back windshield, six of the eight shots cutting the trooper down where he stood. Teflon snatched the gear shift into drive and jumped back onto the highway.

"Treach, are you okay, baby?" she asked in a motherly tone. She had told him to get on the floor and cover his head knowing what Rich intended to do.

"Yes," he answered. Treacherous could feel the glass debris hitting his back as his grandfather launched his assault on the trooper. The shots rang out in his ears like fireworks on the fourth of July. Treacherous was visibly shaken.

"I'm sorry," he heard his grandfather say to his mother.

Rich was not a man of many regrets. However, after the way things were turning out he was starting to regret ever proposing this idea to Teflon. What was supposed to be a full-proof plan was now a disaster. They never anticipated for the worse.

"I told you about talkin' crazy," Teflon replied. "You didn't put a gun to my head or in my hand. I signed up for this shit, remember? We in this together."

Her response was not surprising to Rich.

"Look." She pointed.

"It ends here," Rich retorted, seeing the two state trooper cars zooming on to the interstate.

"Treacherous, stay down," she told her son.

He could tell by her tone another problem had occurred. All that had happened so far seemed surreal to Treacherous. It was like watching a 3-D movie he told himself only with real guns, real people, and real blood.

"We got more company." Rich pointed out. Three more cars traveling south looped around through the grass that divided the interstate.

Teflon had the speedometer to the max. Switching lanes and blowing the horn like a madwoman, Teflon wished Treacherous was there with her.

Her thoughts were interrupted by the sounds of a beep. The gas light appeared on the dashboard as the needle rested on the E. Teflon and Rich exchanged looks without uttering a word. Their silence spoke volumes.

CHAPTER TWENTY

Chief Randle saw the state trooper car up ahead along the shoulder of the interstate and assumed it was the one that had called in the stop. When he didn't see the Avenger alongside the highway, he automatically thought the worse. His thoughts were confirmed as he got close up on the car.

"Fuck," he cursed, seeing the trooper's body on the side of the road.

He immediately picked up the walkie-talkie, radioed it in and floored the gas pedal.

Within minutes, Chief Randle could see the envoy of police cars up ahead. Traffic continued to pull to each side to allow him to pass as his silent siren's light flashed on top of his patrol car. The more the highway parted like the Red Sea, the quicker Chief Randle caught up to the other police cars, passing some along the way.

In no time he could see the back of the royal-blue Dodge Avenger. He could see the Dodge weaving in and out of the traffic up ahead. Seeing the way the car maneuvered caused Chief Randle to reflect on the time he had witnessed the last high-speed chase on WAVY 10 news on this very same highway with the girl and Richard Robinson's son. He wondered what could possibly be going through the minds of the duo he and his colleagues were in pursuit of. His thought came to an end when it looked as if the Dodge

Avenger was stopping.

"This is it." Teflon turned to Rich as the Dodge began to jerk.

She knew they were just mere feet away from being tried, convicted, and sentenced. Just as before when she had found herself in a similar predicament with her other half, although she didn't intend for it to end that way, she was prepared for their final fate. All she could think about was leaving her only child with nothing or no one to love, take care of, and watch over him. Tears of anger began to trickle down her face at the thought.

"Treach, promise me that no matter what, whatever happens you'll stay down," she stated as the car drove its last mile.

"Okay," he replied.

"Promise me."

"I promise," he quickly responded.

"That's my man."

She then redirected her attention to Rich. He appeared to have regained some strength from somewhere, she thought, seeing the familiar look in his eyes. It was the look of a bona fide gangster.

"You ready?" he asked.

"Born ready," she replied.

There was a long pause. Something had been weighing heavy on Rich's mind and heart, and he was undecided on whether he should share it with Teflon or not since he had taken the shots back at the armored truck and even before then. Teflon could see by the expression on his face there was something wrong.

"What's wrong?" She broke the silence.

The question helped Rich make up his mind. "Nothing's wrong," he said. "There's just something I wanted to tell you—something I wanted you to know. I didn't want it to end like this without you knowing."

"Knowing what?" Teflon became impatient seeing Rich was beating around the bush. "Why you talkin' in riddles?" Teflon questioned as the two locked eyes.

Rich let out a half of a chuckle, holding Teflon's stare. He felt like a kid in high school all over again. As hard core and gangster he felt himself to be he couldn't believe how nervous he was. He was more nervous expressing himself than he was about facing the troopers on the highway. Rather than prolong it, he decided to come out and say it.

"I just wanted you to know that I'm in love with—"

The word *you* was silenced by the bullet that penetrated the back of Rich's head. He never got to tell Teflon how he had been secretly in love with her since the first day she had come home from prison. Rich's head landed on Teflon's shoulder. The shot the sharpshooter delivered was responsible for the blood that temporarily dyed her face.

"Nooooo!" she yelled as she attempted to lift him up. "Rich!" Her cries could be heard as she screamed frantically.

The second shot shattered the driver's side window, barely missing her head.

"Ma?" Treacherous rose up and yelled. He had no way of knowing the shots that were to follow ended because of him.

CHAPTER TWENTY-ONE

"Cease fire!" the chief exclaimed. "I repeat, cease fire. This is Chief Randle. There is a child. Abort," he shouted into the walkie-talkie.

From where Chief Randle stood positioned behind his patrol car he was the only senior officer on the scene who had seen the little boy's head surface. He knew the kid was none other than Teflon Jackson's son. The last thing he wanted was for a child to get caught in the crossfire—or worse witness his mother get gunned down right before his very eyes.

"Copy that," the sharpshooter replied. He too now saw the kid in the backseat.

Chief Randle made his way over to the closest officer. "Who's in charge?" he asked.

"Lieutenant Lyles." An officer pointed two cars up to the left.

Chief Randle kept his head low and made his way over to the superior officer on the scene. Hearing that he outranked the officer despite being out of his jurisdiction made him feel more confident with his decision.

"Lieutenant Lyles?" he asked, seeing the gold bar on the lieutenant's shirt.

"What can I do for you?" the lieutenant answered, not bothering to turn around. His focus was on the car ahead.

"I'm Chief Randle. I heard you were in charge here."

"You heard right," the lieutenant replied, now turning toward Chief Randle.

"Well, these particular perps are connected to an armored truck case up 264 I'm heading. Their names are Richard Robinson and Teflon Jackson, both convicted felons, armed robbery charges, both bank jobs. "

"Chief, with all due respect, I appreciate you having my man stand down due to a child being in the vehicle but this is my scene and we got it from here," he said as his eyes shifted back and forth from the chief to the Dodge Avenger.

"I'm not trying to take over here. I'm just lending a helping hand. Correct me if I'm wrong but at the end of the day we do want the best outcome with minimal incident, correct? Now I believe we already have one man down, so lets handle this strategically" Chief Randle expressed.

Lieutenant Lyles studied Chief Randle for a few seconds. "Absolutely, chief," the lieutenant said. "What do you know?"

Chief Randle began to brief the lieutenant on everything he knew about Teflon, Rich, and the case.

CHAPTER TWENTY-TWO

"Treacherous, are you hurt?" Teflon asked as she reclined the seat of the Avenger.

"No." The sound of her son's voice snapped her out of her semi-trance. The shot that had ended Rich's life had come out of nowhere, and all she could think about was his last words before he breathed his last breath. She played them back over and over in her head. She thought she'd heard him wrong but knew she hadn't. She knew now was not the time or place for her to dwell on Rich's words or death, but she didn't have a clue that his feelings for her ran that deep. She was positive she hadn't done anything intentional to fuel his feelings, but at the same time she understood. Teflon shook off his final words but couldn't shake Rich's death. Although they had prepared themselves for the worse, she did not expect Rich to be killed. Her thoughts were moving at lightning speed. She knew her own time was coming to an end and was ready to embrace it, but she couldn't stop thinking about where that would leave her son. Returning to prison was not an option for Teflon. She told herself when she had come home she would rather be carried by six than condemned by twelve. For her prison was the most degrading and worse time of her life. She felt prison was contributing to her animalistic way of thinking and behavior, and that's exactly what she had felt like, a caged animal. Being someone who had always had a problem with authority and taking orders from another she found no pleasure in being told when to eat, sleep, shower, or any other luxuries. The more she thought about it, the more she realized that would be the type of life she'd be subjected to, and once again she'd be leaving her son behind. Thee mere thought upset her. Teflon reasoned with herself that with his bloodline her son was destined to travel the same path she and his father had, and she did not want to take that chance. Just as she made her final decision she heard a voice boom through the bullhorn.

Chief Randle was grateful that Lieutenant Lyles had allowed him to take control of the situation. They knew it was just a matter of time before the Feds arrived on the scene and the both of them lost all control. Coming to an agreement for him to take charge, Chief Randle grabbed the bullhorn.

"Ms. Jackson, this is Chief Randle of the Norfolk Police Department. As you can see we have you surrounded. No one else has to get hurt," he tried to reason. "It doesn't have to end this way. I give you my word if you place your weapons outside of the vehicle and exit the car slowly nothing will happen to you. If not for you, please consider your child," the chief added, attempting to appeal to her maternal side. Remembering the last time she found herself in a similar predicament, Chief Randle knew Teflon Jackson had no problem ending things in the middle of the highway. To his surprise, the driver's door flung open.

"Hold your fire," the chief ordered.

Teflon couldn't help but laugh. The officer was right. It didn't' have to end this way, but it would. Same shit, different day, she thought. She was more than sure that these words were similar to the one's the negotiating officer had offered her and Treacherous the last time she found herself in this similar predicament. She wondered if Treacherous had felt the way she was feeling at that very moment. She reached up and gently brushed her hand across Rich's face.

"Come here, man," she said to Treacherous. "Climb over to me."

A confused Treacherous did as his mother requested. Teflon noticed the manila envelope in her son's hand. She had actually forgotten she had placed the book she had written about her and his father underneath the driver's seat. Seeing the envelope now made Teflon wonder who would write the epilogue, because she knew her final chapter had arrived. With that being her thought, Teflon grabbed hold of the car handle and pushed the door open.

CHAPTER TWENTY-THREE

The first thing Chief Randle saw was the assault rifle hit the pavement when the door of the Dodge opened.

"I can't believe it, chief. You did it," the lieutenant said.

"Not yet," Chief Randle calmly replied. "Everyone, hold your fire," he ordered for a second time. He was fully aware of how riled up officers could get when one of their own had been shot or slain, and he knew all officers on the scene were antsy and itching for one false move on the suspect's part.

Chief Randle watched steadily as Teflon Jackson rose up. He could see a portion of her body appear out of the vehicle. As she carefully made an attempt to climb out of the car the chief noticed the second set of legs that dangled in front of her.

Teflon reached over and grabbed hold of the AR-15. She tossed it out of the car so the authorities could see she was surrendering.

"You gotta trust Mommy on this, okay, baby," Teflon said to her son as she stood up.

"Okay."

"Good. Now stay by Mommy's side and don't let go of me." She half smiled and kissed him on the side of the face.

"No, shoot," she spat back, continuing to approach them.

"Ma, what are you doing?" a scared Treacherous asked..

"Be quiet," was the only response he got.

"Ms. Jackson, please, don't do this. Don't do this to your child," Chief Randle said.

Based on the circumstances he didn't know how much longer he could keep his fellow officers at bay.

"You don't know me. You don't know shit about me or mine," she retorted, pressing the gun even harder against her son's head.

"Okay you're right," he said apologetically. "I don't know you or anything about you, but I know that right now you don't care about dying," the chief added, speaking the obvious. "But what about your son? Don't you care about his life?"

Chief Randle's last words caused Teflon to break out into an insane laughter. He had know idea where her head was at that moment in time.

"What about my son? Do I care about his life?" she repeated with a chuckle.

A bad feeling swept through the chief's body at her words. Not what she had said, but the cynicism and sinister way she'd said them didn't escape him. Where he was once subtle the chief was now in full alert mode.

Tears began to well up in Teflon's eyes as she fought them off. "Son," she started out, "I want you to know that I did this because I love you. I'll see you, Daddy, and Grandpa when I get there," Teflon said all in one breath before she began to apply pressure to the trigger of her Glock 40.

"Hold your fire!" Chief Randle ordered with a wave of his hand as he rushed the two bodies that hit the pavement. The lieutenant and other officers on the scene trailed behind him with their guns drawn. Everything happened so fast no one even knew where the shot had come from.

Chief Randle shook his head in disappointment as he reached the bodies lying on the ground. This was not the way he intended for things to end, but he knew it was a possibility.

"Are you okay?" he asked, kneeling next to the bodies.

Treacherous did not reply. He was still in shock.

Chief Randle grimaced at the sight of Teflon sprawled out on the pavement with her eyes wide open. He had no other choice, he reasoned.

His options were limited, he told himself, as he saw the hole from the shot he fired between her eyes. Either he shot her or he allowed her to shoot her son, and he couldn't let that happen. In the end he had to take a life to spare a life.

"I'm sorry, kid," he offered. "Didn't mean for it to go down like this."

Still Treacherous said nothing. He continued to lay his head on his mother's chest. He didn't have to look up and see the bullet hole between her eyes to know she was dead. He no longer felt her heartbeat or her breathe against his skin. He wept for the loss of his mother as tears soiled his shirt.

Chief Randle rose. He understood the silence from the boy and knew there wasn't anything he could do to console him. Before he knew it every officer and medical team was on the scene. "Can one of you get the boy?" he said, directing his words to one of the EMTs who rushed over, kneeled down, and guided Treacherous away from the body.

"Come on, young man."

Surprisingly, Treacherous did not resist. The paramedic had expected him to throw a tantrum, but he continued to remain silent.

"I don't think he's hurt, but check him out anyway. He may be in shock," Chief Randle instructed just as they had reached the ambulance.

"Sure thing, chief."

"Take it easy," the chief said to Treacherous.

His words caused Treacherous to turn and face him. The chief was taken back by the look that appeared on Treacherous face. "You killed my mother," Treacherous let out. "I won't ever forget you." His words were cold and menacing.

The EMT's eyes widened, but the chief remained calm. The young boy's words were to be expected after all he had just been through and witnessed, the chief thought. He did an about-face and began walking off.

"Chief?" the EMT called out.

When Chief Randle turned around he saw the EMT holding up a manila envelope.

"What do you want me to do with this? I believe the kid had them."

"What's in it?"

The EMT skimmed through the contents of the envelope. "Just some papers. It looks like letters."

"Let him keep it," the chief replied. He figured they were letters written by the boy's mother to him.

He turned back around and started making his way back over to the car. He walked right up on the coroner covering Teflon Jackson's body.

What a tragic day, Chief Randle, thought as he peered into the Dodge Avenger. A total of six bodies had been lost, on the sixth day of the sixth month, 666. It felt like an omen.

So many lives had been taken unnecessarily. The worse part is, the little boy who'd be an orphan for life. Still, this was one case that he no longer had to worry about.

EPILOGUE

Two months later...

"Treacherous it's time to eat," the elderly woman called up to the top of the steps.

Since they had placed him into a new group home in Richmond, Treacherous had isolated and alienated himself from everyone in the facility as much as he could. For the past couple of months all he did was stay in his room and read. The only times he left his room was to eat, shower, or use the bathroom, then he was back to his bed. In a short period he had learned a great deal about his parents through the pages his mother had written. Her death was still fresh in Treacherous' mind, and the incident that lead to her demise began to make sense to him each time he completed a chapter of the story. It became apparent to him that he came from a bloodline of gangsters. It made him feel good to know his parents loved each other and that he wasn't just the result of a mistake and intentionally abandoned. He read in amazement at the type of man and woman his father and mother were. That explained the anger he had built up inside, he realized. The same anger he now harbored for the man named Chief Randle who had killed his mother. That day Treacherous locked in the face of the man responsible for his mother's death. He vowed to himself that the two would cross paths again, and when they did, it would be on his terms.

"Treacherous, we're all waiting on you, dear," the elderly woman called out for a second time.

Treacherous sighed out of irritation. He wanted to finish up the chapter he had just been reading before he went down to eat. He hurried to read the last few sentences that would bring the chapter to an end before he closed the notebook.

Treacherous walked over to where each body lay and lodged another shot into them.

"Let's get the hell up outta here," Pete suggested, snatching up the bag with the drugs and money once Treacherous had reached the final body.

"Nah, you stayin'" Treacherous said to Pete right before he pumped three rounds into his face.

Even I did not expect that, but I was not surprised. I knew my man had good reason. Without me having to ask he said, "I didn't like the way the nigga tried to challenge me in front of you at the rest stop."

I had a feeling that was the case because Pete's words didn't sit right with me either when he told Treacherous he would remember he gave him an invitation for a rematch.

Like always, Treacherous and I made it out in one piece and back to our bikes. We gathered up our belongings, wiped down the motel room and cut our Memorial week short.

Young Treacherous closed the notebook and slipped it under his mattress. As always, he felt a sense of belonging each time he finished reading. Seeing that he was nearly coming to an end of the pages in the second notebook, Treacherous had already made up his mind he would continuing writing where his mother had left off, telling his version of her last days. He couldn't wait until the day when he'd be old enough to pick up where his family had left off. He hoped one day he would find the type of woman his father had in his mother to be his ride or die chick.

Coming Fall 2009

Heaven & Earth

by

J.M. Benjamin

CHAPTER ONE

As Chill turned onto Remsen Avenue in his silver 645i and parked, his eyes immediately zeroed in and locked on Twan. The sounds of So Gangsta off Sam Scarfo's God Don't Like Ugly CD was cut short as Chill shut his Beemer off and hopped out. Chill took a quick glance down at his Black Label hooded sweatshirt, making sure the chrome .45 concealed in his waistband was not bulging. Thinking he had noticed a slight detection of his weapon's presence, Chill smoothed out his hoodie before making a beeline over to Twan.

"Ayo, T, lemme holla at you for a minute," Chill called out, walking up on Twan.

Twan was in the midst of puffing on a blunt of piff when Chill rolled up. Instantly he became agitated by Chill's sudden presence. He was not surprise to see Chill, having a good idea as to why he wanted to speak to him, but he was not in the mood, and he intended to make it known.

"Whatchu wanna holla at me about?" Twan retorted aggressively. "Can't you see I'm busy?" he added, holding the blunt to his mouth, indicating Chill was disturbing his weed smoking session. Chill disregarded Twan's words. A grin appeared across his face as he sighed. He knew confronting Twan was not going to be an easy task, but nonetheless it was long overdue.

"Ayo, Twan, why you keep stepping on my li'l man's toes out here, dawg?" Chill blurted out, catching the attention of everyone within ear-shot.

"I know it's enough paper out here for everybody, son. You ain't gotta be on no cutthroat shit," Chill continued.

After receiving the disturbing phone call that had interrupted him in the middle of something important, it was Chill's intentions to maintain his composure when he confronted Twan, but as he spoke, he could feel his adrenaline stirring up inside. Twan's reaction did little to minimize it.

"Leek, you see this shit? This li'l bitch-ass nigga gonna go run and call his daddy," Twan chimed in disgust, directing his words to one of his street colleagues named Malik with whom he had been sharing the blunt of Purple Haze. Malik made no reaction or gave no indication that he condoned or entertained Twan's remarks. He was cool with both Chill and Twan and remained neutral in the potential altercation as he continued to puff on the blunt Twan had passed him.

"Ain't nobody cut that li'l nigga throat, B," Twan barked in a DMX tone taking offense to Chill's accusation.

"I told that muthafucka that was one of my regulars," he continued in his defense, claiming the drug addict the dispute was over was a personal customer.

This was not the first time Chill and Twan had exchanged words over a drug sale, and Chill was not the only one whose workers had a problem with Twan's tactics in regards to how he hustled on Walnut Ave either. He was just the only one who had stepped to Twan about it. Everyone else was either too afraid of the result of a confrontation with Twan or felt his antics were not affecting their pockets. Chill did not fall into either category. For him, it was merely the principle of the matter. It was about respect—something he felt had diminished a long time ago in the game, but because he was old school, he still gave it, so in return he demanded it.

"Come on, dawg. He told me how shit went down," Chill stated firmly, trying to hide his annoyance with Twan. He had believed all that was relayed to him by one of his workers over the phone prior to his arrival, despite the fact that he had known Twan longer. The only thing knowing Twan longer than his little man accounted for was the fact that Chill knew how Twan got down. He knew Twan was as guilty as sin and had done exactly what he was being accused of doing.

"Yo, he said that fiend nigga didn't even know you, son," Chill revealed, getting fed up with all the word play.

Twan's expression grew cold. "I don't give a fuck what that lil' bitch nigga told you," he quickly snapped. "That was one of my muthafuckin' cuttys, and he wanted to cop from me like I said."

"Yeah, a'ight" Chill replied dryly.

"I know it's a'ight, nigga," Twan said in an attempt to chump Chill off.

Chill caught the sly remark but didn't feed into Twan's attempt. Instead he began to step off seeing that he was actually fighting a lost cause. That is until Twan's next words caused him to pause in his tracks.

"What you need to do is find you some real muthafuckas who can hold their own out here to hustle for you and get rid of them three pussies you got on your team," Twan spit. Chill caught the combination of blatant humor at his expense in Twan's tone, and it had instantly caught his vein. For the life of him he could not understand why his childhood friend was trying to provoke and force his hand. Chill had been in the game for a long time and had been through his share of trials and tribulations in the process and in his opinion had made it through just fine on his own.

No one had ever dictated or schooled him on how to move or conduct his business in the streets, or anywhere else for that matter. He simply learned and taught himself, which is why Twan's words had bothered him so much. He did not take too kindly to someone trying to tell him how to run his operation or handle his B.I., especially someone who knew nothing about running or being a team player.

Chill spun back around. He was now an arm's length away from Twan.

"Don't worry about who the fuck I got on my team or what I'm doin'," Chill said with emphasis, gritting his teeth through clinched jaws.

"Well, nigga, then don't be worried about what the fuck I'm doin then," Twan spit back, "and back the fuck up anyway unless you trynna see me fo' somethin'," he added.

"It's whatever, yo," Chill replied with no intentions of backing down.

"Whoa, whoa, yo, both you niggas chill the fuck out," a kid named Troy intervened. "Niggas trynna eat. Fuck all that other shit, Twan. Go 'head with that, man."

If looks could kill Troy's family would all be dressed in black sobbing over his casket the way Twan had shot him a rock stare.

"Mind ya muthafuckin' business. This don't have nothing to do with you," Twan ordered.

Troy started to respond but thought it best not to comment on Twan's remark. Not while he was without the .40 caliber he normally kept on him. His only intent was to try and defuse the arising altercation between his two street colleagues, but he knew Chill was capable of handling himself in any situation. Troy also knew both men were just alike and neither would back down, which was why he was not surprised when Chill began to speak.

"Yo, ever since you came home from Rahway you think you run shit around here, dawg, but yo, you ain't Debo, kid, and this ain't Friday. You can't keep tryna muscle niggas and think that shit gonna fly," Chill stated sternly. "Them days is over, this is '09, baby."

Chill's words only fueled Twan's fire, which had been slowly igniting inside.

"You say that to say what, dawg? You threatening me or something?" Twan asked with a distorted expression, chest swelling up as his right hand grazed the butt of his gun. He could feel his own adrenaline beginning to kick into overdrive at the thought of what could possibly happen.

Despite him being aware of how everyone viewed him around his hood, Twan knew not everyone on his block feared him, and Chill was one of the ones in that small percentage. And like himself, Twan knew Chill had a reputation for being strapped at all times, not to mention a rep for busting his gun when necessary.

As he towered over Chill's five foot, five inch, 150-pound frame, there was no doubt in his mind that Chill was packing heat. There was no way that Chill would have ever rolled up on him. Not unless he was just plain stupid, had a death wish, or both, Twan thought. No matter what the case, Twan was growing tired of Chill's cockiness and was ready to put an end to the verbal sparing match. In the past he had put hot slugs in dudes for less, but Chill was an exception because they had history. A good one. Before the drug game. But as the situation progressed, Twan was beginning to block all of that out. He was on a mission, and Chill was trying to come in between him and his plight.

"Yo, kid, I don't threaten. All I'm sayin is—"

"Fuck what you sayin', nigga," Twan interrupted in a baritone voice, cutting Chill's words short." I helped pioneer this muthafuckin' block and damn near raised most of you niggas in the game out here. You niggas got drops and all types of trucks and shit while I'm pushin' a old-ass Millennium. Bottom line, I'm doin' what the fuck I wanna do out here until I feel my paper right and if a bitch wanna test me then that's their muthafuckin' funeral. Smell me?" Twan growled, adjusting his hammer in his waistband.

His words drew attention in his direction. Every hustler on the Ave had heard what he had just said and felt some type of way about his statement, but no one dared step up and voice their feelings on the matter. In their minds, each man plotted and anticipated the day they or someone caught Twan slipping. Troy was the only one who was tempted to intervene for a second time, but he thought better of it once again, seeing the visual daggers between Twan and Chill being thrown at each other.

Twan's words tore into Chill like hot slugs. He knew this day would someday come. He had tried his hardest to avoid him and his childhood friends clash. The fact that their was not a person within earshot who wasn't paying attention to what Chill and Twan were saying only heightened the situation because reputations were at stake. Most of the other hustlers were glad that Chill had enough heart to say what they had felt but kept to themselves, while others feared the worse. It was no secret that Twan had come home from East Jersey State Prison, which was one of the roughest prisons in New Jersey six months ago, after serving six years and had been on a paper chase from day one. Originally, he was only supposed to serve four years for the shooting case he went to prison for, but while doing his bid, he stabbed a kid from Camden in the neck in the mess hall over a verbal dispute about a basketball game. The kid survived, but the incident landed him in solitary confinement for two years, and he lost of two years good time, causing him to serve an additional two. The word had spread throughout New Brunswick how Twan from Remsen put work in in the joint and those from his hood knew when he came home he would be the same, if not worse than before. And they were right. Coming home six inches taller and nearly a hundred pounds heavier, Twan tried to flex his muscles, literally, in an attempt to intimidate other hustlers he felt stood in his way of fattening his pockets. He even toted a snub-nosed .44 in his waistband in plain view to let everyone know he stayed strapped. That's why everyone knew he would not let Chill's words ride. His rep depended on it.

Judging by the situation at hand, Chill felt there was no way of getting around it that day. Feeling the tension and knowing both men's caliber, everyone began to fade in an attempt to stand clear of the potential harm. What started out as a minor confrontation was steadily erupting into something major. All eyes were locked on Twan and Chill from a safe distance. Everyone was in fact so focused on the two that no one ever noticed the unidentified SUV parked a short distance up the street...

* * * * * * * * * * * *

The navy blue stolen 2008 Cherokee pulled alongside the curb on Remsen Ave and parked.

"That's him right there," the backseat passenger of the Cherokee pointed out.

"Which one?" the driver asked.

"The big, tall, dark-skinned one with the velour sweat suit on."

"It don't even matter which one he is," the front seat passenger interjected.

"It ain't like these niggas out here gonna just let us walk up on their man and do something to him, then just walk up outta here."

"I was thinking the same thing," the driver said.

"So what are we gonna do?" the backseat passenger asked.

"You ain't gonna do shit, you gonna stay ya ass in the truck while we handle this shit. If he see ya ass, he gonna remember you."

"Look," the driver said to the front seat passenger. "Something about to go down."

The front seat driver immediately drew attention to the commotion.

"Not without us it ain't," the front seat passenger said, snatching open door just before pulling the black mask over their face.

"Get behind the wheel and be on point," the driver instructed the backseat passenger, doing the same with their mask before exiting the SUV to back up their partner.

"Yo, T, you must think shit sweet, dawg," Chill said, standing his ground. "Ain't nothing pussy about me, kid, so all that shit you poppin' is extra. Ain't nobody trynna test you, big homie. Niggas know how you get down, but just like I know you not gonna let a bitch carry you like a sucka, you gots to know that neither am I. So, what are we gonna do? Huh? Shoot each other over a punk-ass hundred-dollar sale 'cause I got my strap on me, too, daddy," Chill informed Twan, lifting the Black Label hoodie up enough to reveal his .45 automatic.

"And if you reach for ya joint, that's exactly what's gonna happen, my nigga," Chill added, giving fair warning. He had hoped Twan used what little sense he had given him the benefit of doubt for having and saw the bigger picture, causing him to make the right decision. The last thing Chill wanted was to catch a body or get bodied over a petty drug dispute. But he knew in the streets people had killed and died for less so he was prepared for whatever.

Twan grilled him intensively while pondering over his words. He knew himself all too well and knew without a doubt if he pulled his gun he wouldn't hesitate to use it, but the two things that weighed on his mind the most were one, was he ready to go back to the one place he despised the most and two, would he actually be able to beat Chill to the draw? It was those two reasons and them alone that caused Twan to make his decision to let sleeping dogs lie. For the moment anyway, but he made a mental note and a promise to himself that he would finish what Chill had started some other time.

"Fuck that one hundred dollars," Twan spit, reaching into his pocket.

A small load had been lifted off Chill's shoulders. At first, Chill thought Twan was reaching for his gun and was about to reach for his own until he saw that was not the case. Instead, Twan pulled out a knot of cash. "Here, take this shit," he said, tossing a hundred-dollar bill in Chill's direction.

Insulted by the gesture, Chill instantly replied, "Man, I don't want ya money, kid."

In all honesty it wasn't about the money at all with Chill, but Twan did not get it. He now also felt insulted by Chill's decline.

"Oh, my paper ain't good e—"

"What the—"

"Oh shit!"

"Somebody call a muthafuckin' ambulance!" Troy shouted.

The sound of Troy's voice caused Chill to end his pursuit.

"Yo, who the fuck was that?" an out-of-breath Chill asked, making his way back to where shots had moments ago erupted, with .45 still in hand. He had just chased and unloaded his clip on the navy blue Cherokee in the middle of his block, and the two masked gunmen jumped in and sped off. He watched as the Cherokee's tail lights vanished up the street.

"I don't know, but Twan's hit," a bewildered Troy yelled.

By then, everyone had come out of their hiding places and surrounded Twan.

His body laid helplessly on the ground as blood spilled out of his mouth and seeped out of his bullet-riddled body. Countless shots ripped into his flesh before he even had the chance to pull his weapon.

He could hear the voices surrounding him, asking questions to no avail. The only one who was able to provide them with answers was Twan himself, but the blood that began to clog his throat prevented him from speaking out as he lay there fighting for his life. He made an attempt to speak but had only managed to grunt inaudibly. He could not believe—or rather, didn't want to believe—this was his final fate. During his time in prison, he had heard so many stories about other brothers getting out after serving years and years on lock down, going home in search of their ghetto forty acres and a government mule only to have their lives cut short from making the mistake of underestimating a person's capabilities. Now here it was he was faced with the same type of statistical situation from making that same fatal error.

As his life began to flash before his very eyes, he couldn't help but to think about how he had gone around the drug block the other day, smacking up and robbing the young pretty girl who had bruised his ego by rejecting him. He would have let the matter ride until the girl had added insult to injury by pulling more money out of her pocket than Twan, after he'd tried to impress her with a baller demeanor. And now, it was because of his egotistical way of thinking that he had gotten more than what he'd bargained for. And because he'd reacted first without thinking, he now felt the unfortunate wrath of Heaven and Earth.

That being his last thought, Twan's eyes dilated as his body convulsed. Death had opened its door and embraced him before the ambulance arrived.

CHAPTER TWO

"Le-Le, slow the fuck down," Earth commanded from the backseat of the Cherokee, pulling off her mask. "You gonna get us knocked the fuck off."

Glancing at the speedometer, Le-Le did as she was told. She hadn't realized she was doing eighty miles per hour up Commercial Avenue. Her only concern was getting her two girlfriends out of harm's way after the gun battle jumped off on the notorious drug block. There was no way she would have been able to live with herself if something was to have happened to either of them. After all, it was because of her they had gone around the drug block in the first place.

"Are y'all alright?" Le-Le asked, looking back at them through the rearview mirror.

"Yeah, we good," Heaven assured her, "but I can't say the same for that joker."

"So y'all got 'em then?"

"Fuck you mean did we get 'em? Of course we did," Earth spat irritably.

"Cool out," Heaven said, attempting to calm her. She knew where the hostility was coming from and didn't blame her, but now was not the time for either of them to lose a level head.

"Nah. Fuck that," Earth retorted, not wanting to let the matter go. "We wouldn't even be in this predicament if it weren't for this bitch. I told ya dumb ass before about showing off for muthafuckas.",She directed her words at Le-Le.

"I wasn't trynna—"

"Just shut the fuck up and drive," Earth said, cutting her off.

Heaven knew better than to intervene when Earth was reprimanding one of their workers. Not only were she and Earth partners in crime, but they had been friends even longer, so Heaven knew her girl all too well. There was no doubt in her mind if she continued to try and pacify the situation or aid Le-Le in any type of way, it would only add fuel to the fire. Earth had been that way for as long as Heaven could remember, extending back to their days when the two had first met at Edna Mahan Correctional Facility for Women in Clinton, New Jersey. As Earth continued to scold and verbally chastise Le-Le, Heaven could not help but reflect on their first encounter.

2000...

"Listen up for your name. State your number when your name is called."

It had been six long and stressful months in Middlesex County's jail, and Heavenly Devine Jacobs was finally being shipped out to prison. She was more than ecstatic. First time ever being locked up, Heavenly had copped out to a plea agreement of seven years with a three-and-a-half stipulation, all for the sake of love. At least that's what she had thought at the time.

Growing up in New Brunswick, New Jersey, raised by her father, who was known to be one of the biggest heroin dealers in town and a mother who was deemed one of the baddest females in all of Franklin, Heavenly's childhood was that of a ghetto fairy tale.

At birth, she had inherited her mother's God-given beauty but as she grew older she gravitated and inherited her father's taste for the streets and money. By the time she was fifteen, Heavenly, who had shortened her name to Heaven, had every baller, young and old alike, who laid eyes on her wanting her for themselves. But only those who had paper and plenty of it could afford the luxury, and even then Heaven made it hard for them because her father saw to it that she wanted for nothing—that is until an uneventful day that changed Heaven's life forever.

When she was eighteen, Heaven's parents were murdered during a home invasion over money and drugs, while Heaven was away partying in Cancun with friends.

Having practically been left with nothing, Heaven instantly switched into survival mode, using her knowledge of the game and her most valuable assets to get ahead in life. In no time, she had secured the position of wifey/ride or die chick with a known money getter named Screw from Troop Ave.

Initially Heaven's intent was to do what she had to do in order to survive, but as time progressed she found herself falling in love with Screw. It was that same love that caused her to take the weight for two hundred fifty grams of coke and one hundred grams of dope that was found during a raid in an apartment in her name. Heaven was convinced Screw loved her just the same if not more, which was why she didn't hesitate to step up to the plate and wear the drugs when Screw had asked her to. Screw had constantly and continuously showed his love and support to Heaven, making sure her commissary was strapped, accepting her collect calls, never missing a visit or court date, and sending letters and cards daily. Screw had done everything any woman in Heaven's position would want a man to do for her all the way up to the time Heaven had signed on the dotted line and was sentenced on her plea. She couldn't believe how naive she had been fallen victim to love knowing her parents, more so her father had taught her better. The entire time Heaven assumed her man was keeping it real with her like she was with him, but he was keeping it real fake. As if like magic, Screw vanished, leaving Heaven with a lengthy prison bid and a hardened heart.

"Heavenly Jacobs."

"400441," Heavenly replied.

This was the number that was given to her after sentencing—a number she had memorized and would remember for the rest of her life. In the six months she had been confined, incarceration had already began to impact on her life. Bitter, she vowed to leave out better and smarter than when she had come in. Only in Heaven's case, she was set on becoming a better and smarter criminal. Heaven peered out of the gated window of the NJDOC bus as it arrived and came to a halt at the state's women correctional facility. When it was her turn to exit what was called the Blue Bird, an eerie feeling swept through her.

No more than five minutes inside the Clinton women's prison, women of all shades, weights, and heights filled the dayroom. When she and others entered the housing unit that would be her place of residency for the next three years or so, she knew she was going to have problems. She heard someone catcall "fresh meat" as she and five other women carefully walked down the tier with bedrolls in hand in search of their assigned cells. Other women began to pour out into the dayroom from their cells hearing the fresh meat call. It was apparent two of the females who had been shipped with Heaven had been to the facility before. Heaven noticed they were giving handshakes and hugs to a few of the women and overheard one of them ask what they done this time to return. While she continued down the tier in search of her cell, Heaven also peeped three manly looking females eyeing her from afar, but she did her best to maintain her poker face and pretend she hadn't noticed.

After only a week at the facility, the same trio who Heaven realized were female studs tried to run up in her cell with the intentions of conducting a gang rape. Heaven was no slouch when it came to throwing her hands, but she was not sure if she could fight off the three brawly butch chicks. Ready to defend her womanhood or die trying, Heaven positioned her back against the cell's wall, threw her hands up, and got in a fighting stance. The three would-be rapers all smiled.

"Bitch, we can do this the easy way or the hard way," the biggest of the three said in a deep tone, unfazed by Heaven's attempt to defend herself. The other two females barricaded the entrance of the cell with their huge, grotesque bodies while their partner prepared to make her move. Just as the gorilla of a woman was about to launch her attack, a shadow over swept the six-by-nine cell from behind them all. Heaven had also noticed the sudden dimness but couldn't see the cause.

When the three would-be rapers all turned and directed their attention toward the cell's entrance, their eyes widened at the sight of Earth who stood just outside of the cell's doorway in her white wife beater, gray sweatpants, and beige state boots tightly tied, twirling two razor blades around in her mouth with her tongue. With the exception of the battle scars illuminating from her forehead, her deep chocolate complexion glistened from the petroleum jelly that lightly covered her face, toned shoulders, upper chest, and folded muscular arms as she posted up. She had watched from day one when the pretty, long-haired, voluptuously shaped red bone had come into the institution, and Teresa and her clique immediately began scoping her out.

Normally she didn't get involved in other people's affairs, but there was something about the new girl that drew Earth in, besides the fact that she had a weakness for light-skinned women.

Well aware of Earth's reputation with the two infamous blades she always kept in her mouth, the two girls who posed as blockers for the intended rape stood down. Neither of the two wanted any problems with Earth, but Teresa's ego and pride took control over her intellect. She could not let Earth punk her, especially not in front of her two lovers.

"Yo, this don't have nuthin' to do with you, E. You don't know nuthin', you don't see nuthin', won't be nuthin', ya dig," Teresa spat boldly.

Earth unfolded her arms, ran her right hand across her beehive waves, and snickered to herself. Teresa's words held no weight. She had known her for years, even outside the prison walls. They were both from Plainfield—Earth from the projects, Teresa from Third Street. That was like mixing oil and water where they came from. Earth believed Teresa to be a coward who preyed on who she felt to be the weak on the streets, and she had been displaying the same behavior at the facility since Earth had come. The two didn't get along on the outside and the same applied on the inside. Up until that moment, Teresa had stayed out of Earth's way and never gave her a reason to pull her card or go up against her. That day Earth welcomed the challenge.

The last female who had made the mistake of going against her had received more zippers on her face than Edward Scissorhands, resulting in Earth serving nine months in lockup. Without uttering so much as one word, the two other females cautiously began to bail out of the cell like a row of ducks, not even attempting to glance over at Earth out of fear of triggering her. They saw what was evolving between Earth and Teresa. Though they were Teresa's lovers, they knew the three of them combined were no match for Earth. On several occasions they were all too familiar with her work with both her hands and the razors. The two did not want to risk leaving prison with any additional marks than when they had come in the facility. Earth had already envisioned the cut she intended to carve into Teresa's face. She could see in Teresa's eyes that she was ready to make her move. Just as Earth was about to spit out the blade and commence to cutting, Heaven landed a right hook that connected with Teresa's jaw. Though the punch didn't send her to the canvas, it was effective enough to give Heaven the upperhand. Seeing that she was dazed, Heaven grabbed a fistful of Teresa's cornrows and threw what seemed like a hundred punches in succession into her face.

"New booty, chill," Earth repeated for the umpteenth time, but her words fell on deaf ears. It took four officers and a direct hit of pepper spray to the face for Heaven to discontinue the beat down she had been giving Teresa. Heaven received ninety days in lockup and returned to her initial unit while Teresa was transferred.

Not knowing her motives at the time, as soon as she spotted Earth she approached her. "Thanks, but I could've handled that."

"I'm sure you could've, and you did," was all Earth replied before walking off.

Two days went by before either of the two said anything else to each other. It was Heaven again who had approached Earth.

"For what it's worth, I appreciate you having my back that day."

"It's cool."

"They call me Heaven," she said.

"Earth." They both gave knowing grins at the irony of their names.

"Despite where we are, nice to meet you." Heaven extended her hand.

"Yeah, no doubt." Earth gave her a handshake. She noticed how soft Heaven's hand felt and drew her own back, not wanting to give off the wrong impression.

Heaven lowered her hand. She had a strong idea why Earth had broken free of their introductory handshake. There was no doubt in Heaven's mind that like her attackers, Earth's sexual preference was the same sex, but her demeanor seemed genuine, and Heaven respected that.

"If you ever need anything, don't hesitate to ask," Heaven offered.

"Back at you," was Earth's response. That day a seed was planted.

Within a few months Heaven and Earth became tighter than spandex, · forming a bond as thick as thieves. No one could utter a word, look at, or even breathe funny around Heaven without facing consequences at the hands of Earth. She had pounded a female from Elizabeth unconscious just for commenting to someone that she felt Heaven thought she was all of that. She ended up serving another six months in lockup for that. The incident caused everyone, including the officers, to believe Heaven and Earth were lovers, but that was far from the case. They were more like sisters than anything, and whenever Earth was not in the hole, their discussions and plans extended far beyond sexuality. Even then, they managed to stay in touch, plot, and plan through letters and messages passed on by cool officers and trustees who frequented and worked the ad-seg unit. As beautiful as Heaven was and despite the fact that Earth had a thing for thick red bones, she had the utmost respect for Heaven and never came at her on that order. It was that same respect that had spilled over into the streets when the two had been released from prison.

-Stay Tuned

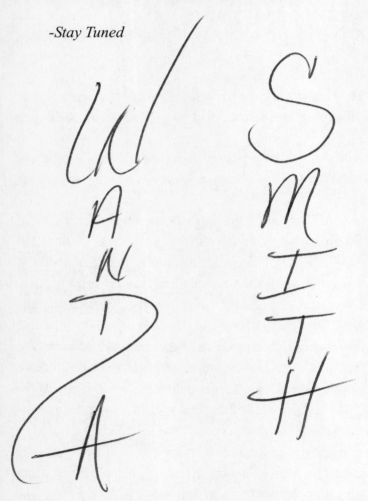

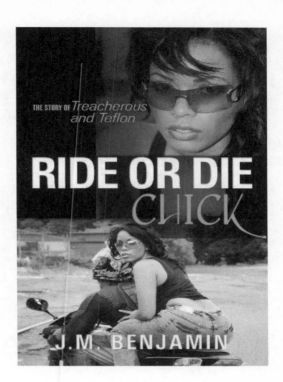

Life isn't easy for Treacherous or Teflon, but when this modern day Bonnie & Clyde duo hook up life won't be easy for anyone seeing paper in Virginia. Bonded by tragic childhoods Treacherous and Teflon grew up hard on the streets of VA. But those same Virginia streets will be suffering losses as ballers from VA or others just visiting the city fall victim to Treach and his Ride or Die chick Teflon!

With their murderous robbing spree sparing no one just how long can Treach and Teflon continue to terrorize the streets of Virginia before they fall victim to the streets again? Can Treach and his murder Mami, Teflon come out on top?

Ride or Die Chick, The Story of Treacherous and Teflon is about two people who come from nothing and are willing to do whatever it takes to obtain everything.

This is a modern day tale of Bonnie & Clyde and built on a love that is stronger than that of Romeo and Juliet. A bonafide gangster, Treacherous is confident that he can't lose, as long as he has his ride or die chick!

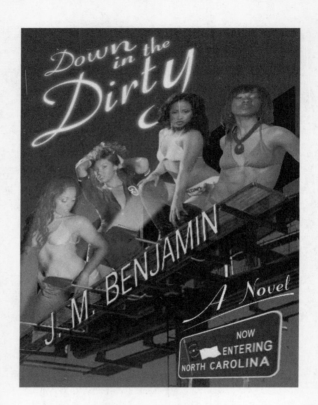

Childhood friends, Keisha, Desiree, Tasha, and Pam quickly learn how to use their beauty and sexual prowess to manipulate men. Each woman has suffered abuse at the hand of a man and they decide to make a life-long pact to get revenge on ballas. These gorgeous but scandalous women turn the tables by making men who cross their path, especially if their not from the dirty, pay for their womanizing behavior.

After pulling several heists and getting away with murder, these ruthless and cold-hearted women will stop at nothing to get what they want—until one of them begins to fall for her prey.

"J.M. Benjamin's freshman novel is pure fire! *Down in the Dirty* takes urban literature to a new high."

–Nikki Turner, national bestselling author of *Hustler's Wife* and *The Glamorous Life*

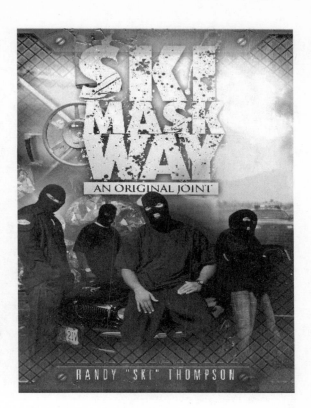
"An intriguing story of a young man's struggle with morality and a quest for fast cash."
    —K'wan, Essence #1 bestselling author of Hood Rat *and* Still Hood

Isaiah "Ski" Thompson is a young man who plans to get his family out of the 'hood with his basketball skills, but when he goes to college and things don't turn out the way he hoped, he trades in his hoop dreams for street dreams.

Ski and six of his childhood friends, The Go-Hard Crew, go on a robbing spree across New York State—no one and no place of business is off limits. After a botched robbery claims the life of one of his best friends, and he finally finds true love, Ski vows to change his life and return to school. Making fast money comes with a high penalty, and Ski quickly learns that once the streets get a grip on you, it's hard to break loose.

POLE
POSITION
A NOVEL
ARNOLD
DORSEY-BEY

Casablanca is the hottest strip joint in Maryland, featuring the baddest chicks on the East coast. The seven deadly sins are served on a platter. Casablanca enters the annual Pole Position Competition where there's one million dollars at stake, and a place that already breeds envy takes a turn for the worse. The women will stop nothing to win the championship.

Meet Sampson and Delilah, the top billing acts at Casablanca. Can the love that this couple shares transcend the barriers of the underworld? When money, mayhem, and murder threaten to ruin the reputation of Casablanca, and the love of Samson & Delilah all parties involved must pray to the hustlas god…

Whatever happens in Casablanca stays in Casablanca!

INTRODUCTION BY **ZANE**

Steamy Erotic Stories

TWILIGHT MOODS

Edited by **Jossel Flowers Green**

LIMITED EDITION

Twilight Moods is the first independent novel to bring you stories from a dazzling array of today's hottest authors. Prepare yourself because your temperature will rise as Timmothy B. McCann gives it to you "Fuller, Deeper, Smoother" while Joylynn M. Jossel wants to know if you've been "Daydreaming at Night" and Sandra A. Ottey helps you start your workday with her "Blue-Collar Love." Lolita Files spices up lunch with a little "Bobby Q's Sauce." Rochelle Alers steams up the evening with a hot and seductive "Anniversary."

Introduction by Zane, the New York Times bestelling of Addicted, *The Sex Chronicles, Gettin' Buck Wild, The Heat Seekers, The Sisters of APF, Shame on It All, Nervous, Skyscraper, Afterburn,* and *Love Is Never Painless* and is also the editor of *Chocolate Flava* and *Caramel Flava.*

Submission Guidelines

Flowers in Bloom Publishing is pleased to receive query letters for fiction manuscripts, including those for novels, contemporary, urban, inspirational and motivational. WE DO NOT ACCEPT WORKS OF POETRY. We do not accept handwritten materials and do not offer typing services. Queries should include a typed cover letter, author background and publication history (if applicable), a detailed synopsis of the proposed work, and a sample chapter. Please indicate if the work is simultaneously submitted.

FLOWERS IN BLOOM PUB. is an independent house, we accept only a very small percentage of the works proposed to us. Since the size of our editorial staff reflects the size of the company on the whole, we ask that you be patient while we consider your work. Our aim is to respond to proposals as quickly as possible, and to requested manuscripts within two months. While we appreciate the interest of all of the dedicated writers who propose and submit their work to us, we can't always adhere to set time frames, or provide as comprehensive a response to the works as we would like.

Please download our **manuscript submission form** from our website at www.flowersinbloompublishing.com.

Please include a self-addressed, stamped business envelope for our response to your query, and a self-addressed, stamped mailer if you would like your materials to be returned. Please do not send original artwork or irreplaceable documents as we cannot assume responsibility for these.

Send to:

Flowers In Bloom Publishing
2152 Ralph Avenue #421
Brooklyn, New York 11234

Attn: MS DEPT